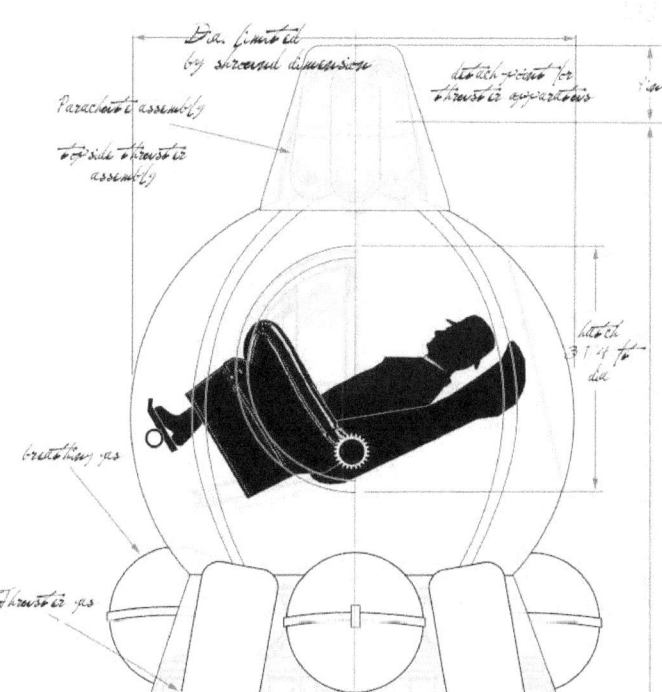

The Sun Never Sets

Cate Caldwell
Matt Pearson

Grey Wolfe Publishing, LLC
PO Box 1088
Birmingham, Michigan 48009
www.GreyWolfePublishing.com

© 2014 Cate Caldwell
© 2014 Matt Pearson
Published by Grey Wolfe Publishing, LLC
www.GreyWolfePublishing.com
All Rights Reserved

FIRST EDITION ISBN: 978-1628280470
SECOND EDITION ISBN: 978-1628281545
Library of Congress Control Number: 2014949328

Grey Wolfe Publishing LLC
Ui bona na corbin

The Sun Never Sets

Cate Caldwell
Matt Pearson

Acknowledgements:

First and foremost, we would like to acknowledge Narayana Swamy, whose feedback undoubtedly improved the quality of the book.

We would also like to acknowledge Evelyn Zimmer, who lent her keen eye and careful editing skills to the novella.

Finally, we'd like to acknowledge all our friends, family and colleagues who have read our work, attended readings, or simply encouraged us to keep writing.

Thank you all. May the Force be with you.

Prologue

German East Africa, 1899

Hiram Codon had long maintained that there was only one thing more out of place than an Englishman in Africa, and that was a German trying to emulate an Englishman in Africa. He was reminded of this by six such Germans who were rapidly gaining on him and his young assistant even as he pushed his steam carriage to its limits. The machine protested with a cacophony of hisses, clanks and whines of stressed metal as it bounded down the dusty road travelling barely faster than the pursuing horses.

And then the shooting started.

Hiram was distracted from the panicked shriek of his assistant by the curious sensation of wind passing over his head.

"Compose yourself, William," Hiram shouted, his authoritative brogue carrying over the noise of his steam carriage and the German guns behind them. "It's just a bowler." It had, however, been Hiram's favorite hat.

"They're shooting at us!" William shouted as though it were informative. He was young, of an age that would have been optimal for military service in a man of sterner mettle. As it was, William was well suited to his clerical duties in the relative comfort of the office, but in the field he was unflatteringly prone to hysterics.

Hiram hunched forward over the steering column in an effort to keep his head low. German bullets punched into the wooden body of the carriage and ricocheted off the metal, adding to the chaotic orchestra of their escape. William again voiced his panic.

"Stop cowering like a hedgehog," Hiram commanded as he grabbed one of several levers protruding from the side of his seat. The trunk behind their seats popped open as a balloon inflated from a pressurized tank no larger than a man's forearm. The rising balloon carried with it a radio apparatus of copper, wood and glass which rose remarkably unscathed through the hail of bullets and shotgun pellets chipping at the carriage.

"Gunter! Can you hear me?" Hiram shouted into the wood-framed microphone clutched in his hand. William, who had been feeding the wire as the balloon ascended, ducked back to cover as the rapidly gaining Germans sent shards of blasted wood splintering from the rear of the carriage with a rain of buckshot.

Preoccupied with driving and operating the radio, Hiram failed to notice the small trunk that tumbled from the shattered rear of the carriage, spilling its contents onto the roadside. The Germans, equally oblivious, rode past the brass and steel sphere as it rolled into the brush. The device, a gyroscope built under contract by associates of Doctor Gunter Wolfe, Hiram's partner, was the source of the present misunderstanding.

"Who is with—" Hiram's handset squawked in a shrill German-accented voice before hissing to static. Glass and wood shreds rained down on his hatless head.

"We are almost upon you!" Hiram shouted into the microphone.

"Death is almost upon us," William shrieked, cowering as far under his seat as he could manage.

"Bollocks," Hiram muttered as he brushed the detritus of wood and vacuum tubes from himself with his free hand. The Germans were by now only a few paces behind, thanks to the damage they'd inflicted on the carriage and the drag from the balloon that now trailed behind uselessly. He smiled broadly as the carriage rumbled past a prospectors' camp, on toward a ramshackle pier that pointed the way toward a steamship waiting in the harbor.

"Fortune smiles at last," Hiram gloated, before a high-pressure pipe burst with a thunderous crack and scalding steam spewed in a flowering geyser from the carriage. "Like a syphilitic whore," Hiram added as he struggled to regain some semblance of control over the machine.

High-pressure steam shot out of the maze of pipes beneath their seats, accompanied by the metallic tinging of bullet impacts. The carriage coughed and jolted with deceleration until Hiram disengaged the clutch, hoping momentum would carry it.

Flames erupted from beneath the boiler, which spewed its contents in a searing mist that had the one virtue of slowing the horses of their pursuers.

Hiram had no time to comment unfavorably on William's undignified scream as the carriage, engulfed in flame, clattered down the pier before toppling over the end into the ocean.

Hiram hit the water like a rhino dropped from a dirigible, making up for lack of grace with the authority of the impact. He wiped his eyes just in time to catch sight of the round life preserver spinning through the air toward him. He was almost able to avoid being hit, but not quite. He suspected, rightly so, that Gunter had thrown it at him on purpose.

"Climb aboard," Gunter shouted from the deck of the ship. The taunting laugh that followed did not go unnoticed.

"You are a madman!" William shouted, flailing his arms and splashing Hiram with every panicked swing. "Find someone else to manage your lunacy! I quit!"

Hiram ignored him. He pulled himself onto the life preserver and swam toward the ship. The Germans showed no interest in fishing them from the water, being content to recover the remaining contents of the half-submerged carriage.

One final shot from a German rifle startled Hiram as he swam. He turned, hoping it hadn't been meant for him, and saw the antenna balloon flutter sadly to the water, having been punctured by a well-placed shot.

"Bollocks," he muttered. Such had been the entire expedition.

Chapter

Kolkata, India, 1899

Ravi Mukherjee disliked pageantry as much as the populace was purported to love it. Even a casual observer might have guessed this about the young man, who was tidily and conservatively dressed in a gray coat with covered buttons, matching waistcoat, dark trousers, short turnover shirt collar, and bow tie.

He thrummed his fingers on his impeccably organized desk and glowered moodily at a ledger. One of his employees, Sri Ganguli, who sat at the desk closest to his, watched him.

For the past several months, Ravi had done nothing but plan for the new Viceroy's arrival in India, which entailed travel arrangements not only for the incoming Viceroy, Lord Curzon, but also for the departing Viceroy, Lord Elgin, as well as a plethora of foreign dignitaries. He had directed the decorations along the carriage route and made arrangements for the rifle salutes. He had coordinated with civil, military and government offices, as well as the local princes.

As one of a small minority of Indians in the Indian Civil Service, Ravi knew he should be grateful for the opportunity. However, it seemed to him like a massive expenditure of both resources and manpower that could be put to better use. It was as if the Raj weren't aware of the cholera epidemic, or the famine happening in the north.

This was not entirely fair, Ravi knew. There were some attempts to mitigate the damage, but they could not lay railroad track or dig canals quickly enough to get resources to everyone in need. Five years ago, when he had just finished college and passed the ICS entrance exam, Ravi had written a paper proposing a solution. A rather good one, he thought.

Dirigibles. Airships for delivery of goods to the countryside. This solution would require no new infrastructure beyond the ships themselves, and they could touch down virtually anywhere in rural India.

Unfortunately, he seemed to be the only person who thought this was a good idea. His superiors scoffed at him, saying 'they do not make deliveries by airship in London.'

"Perhaps," Ravi had countered, "that is because in London there is not enough space to land airships."

But of course, the way it is done in London is the way it should be done everywhere, whether or not the environment is completely different. Also, as a colonial, and a non-white one at that, his ideas were less likely to be taken seriously.

So, here he was, trying to arrange for elephants for the new Viceroy's arrival. This entailed negotiating with one of the neighboring princely states. Its maharaja, however, was proving to be quite impossible. Each time Ravi had attempted to meet with the man, he had been so deep in his cups he could barely speak. Last time Ravi had visited the palace, the maharaja was nowhere to be found. His eldest son tried to negotiate in his stead, but the spoiled prince had the attention span of a spider monkey. He left the table to chase one of the maids.

Ravi had attempted to report the difficulties to his immediate superior, Major Maxwell Cullen, but he could not find Cullen, either. Ravi had attempted to contact him at home, where he was greeted warmly—uncomfortably so, in fact— by Cullen's wife Elizabeth, who eventually informed him that her husband was off hunting tigers.

While studying in London, Ravi had heard stories of patients at the Bethlehem Royal Hospital, commonly known as Bedlam. The antics of the government officials reminded him of nothing so much as anecdotes from the madhouse. He was surrounded by crazy people.

Ravi lifted his head, making eye contact with Sri.

"Sri, cross off the elephants from the procession list."

"Mister Mukherjee?" Sri asked.

"Just do as I ask. Elephants are not necessary," Ravi reiterated.

"I'm told," Sri said carefully, "That Lord Curzon loves elephants. As well as ceremony."

"I'm also told he is fond of efficiency. We are already over budget with this event," Ravi said peevishly.

Sri raised his eyebrows, made a note in a ledger, and left the room.

That, thought Ravi, *is that*. He did not understand the fascination with elephants as part of ceremonies, with hanging tapestries and jewelry off them and making them walk in a line. He preferred the beasts as they were in the wild, behaving according to their natures.

Perhaps, thought Ravi, *it is because the British government in India somewhat resembles an elephant—huge, ponderous, meandering at a moderate pace toward some uncertain goal.*

He wondered if anything would change with the new Viceroy's arrival. Though Curzon was, purportedly, the first Viceroy of India who had actually wanted the job, Ravi still had his doubts.

****

Carriages were lined up along the street bordering Dalhousie square, signaling the end of the work day. The breeze, blowing in from the direction of the Hooghly River, tousled the leaves of the banyan, mango and palm trees, spicing the air with a lush aroma. Ravi hailed a Hansom cab, and nodded to the driver as he climbed inside.

In the mild January weather, even on a sunny day, Ravi was glad for his British-style clothing. Admittedly, Ravi was seldom too warm, even in the heavy, humid heat of summer. He could happily wear trousers and a waistcoat in July, while many of his British counterparts found Kolkata summers disagreeable. They sweated buckets in their western attire, which Ravi found moderately amusing. The British officers would no more wear native-style dress in India, comfortable or no, than Ravi would walk around London in a dhoti.

Ravi had been as uncomfortably cold in London as the British officers were uncomfortably warm, here. And though London had much to recommend it, it was not the paradise he had been led to expect. He had somehow thought England would be populated entirely by gentlemen and ladies, as silly as that sounded to him, now. On the contrary, he had been taken aback by the crushing poverty in certain areas of the city, and by the crime.

The cab driver pulled up in front of Ravi's apartments. Ravi tipped him, waved to a group of dhoti-clad children playing in the street, and mounted the stairs.

Ravi's apartments were modest, but tastefully appointed. He hung his waistcoat on a rack in the sitting room, brushing it off. The primary feature of the room was a mahogany desk, which was as compulsively well-ordered as his work space. Bookshelves lined two walls of the room, and a small sitting space with a comfortable chair, lamp, and small table were arranged opposite. The fourth wall was covered mostly with windows.

On the desk sat a lion. A Roullet and Decamps clockwork automaton, which a friend from school had bought for him while on holiday in Paris. Ravi peered into the marble eyes of the cat, and then removed a key from a desk drawer and wound it up. Clicking, like a child's teeth chattering, or a swarm of angry insects, the lion drew itself back on its haunches and then pounced at Ravi.

Ravi was glad it still worked, considering he had immediately taken it apart and reassembled it. It had occurred to him that wasn't a nice thing to do with a gift, but he'd been too curious not to.

Maybe someday they will build enormous clockwork elephants, Ravi thought. That way, they could drape rugs all over them and make them be part of ceremonies without annoying the real beasts.

A couple of other whimsical curiosities stood out in the mostly stately, and somewhat stodgy, sitting room. A toy helicopter designed by Alphonse Penaud. A portrait of a colorful hot air balloon.

It suddenly occurred to Ravi that, were he to leave tomorrow never to return, he wouldn't miss a thing in his home other than this ridiculous clockwork lion and an equally absurd flying whirly-bird.

What good is it to be melancholy? Ravi chided himself. There was too much to do, what with the new Viceroy coming tomorrow. He went into the kitchen to prepare some tea. It was likely to be a long night.

****

Ravi would have liked a bird's-eye view of the procession. From a balloon or airship, the line of carriages through the decorated streets, the crowds on rooftops, the troops lining every street along the route must have been very impressive, indeed. They heard the first rifle salute echoing from the ramparts of Fort William.

Ravi was in front of the government house attending to last minute logistics. The Lieutenant Governor waited at the foot of the grand staircase, while two distinct military regiments waited to provide a second welcoming rifle salute. Foreign dignitaries and Indian nobles from princely states all over the country spoke in low, but excited tones.

He was just thinking that the event was going as well as he could have hoped, with no last minute difficulties, when one voice began to rise above the ambient conversations. One that became increasingly shrill. One that Ravi recognized.

Other voices began to drop off, as guests swiveled their heads to locate the source of the dreadful row.

"How dare you come in here making such accusations? You think you can just walk into someone else's country and do or say whatever you want?" snapped Elizabeth Cullen. "Bloody Americans."

The irony was not lost on Ravi. He approached her and the American, who looked wholly taken aback.

"Ah, Ravi," she said. "You simply must eject this—" Elizabeth looked the man up and down, as if unable to come up with a sufficient insult to describe him.

"Missus Cullen, why don't we step over here into the shade for a moment. Perhaps I can get you a little water, or even a glass of wine?"

"I don't want a drink, I want this man out! Out, out, out!"

Tentatively, Ravi reached out to take Elizabeth's arm. Her eyes flashed, and for a moment Ravi thought he'd made a terrible mistake, that he was next in line for a deluge of Elizabeth's venom. Then the anger seemed to go out of her.

"Come, now," he said, leading her away from the crowd.

On the other side of the building, there were fewer spectators, and these had their backs to them. Ravi walked Elizabeth to the shade of a large tree and handed her a small fan. She immediately started fanning herself.

"The nerve of some people," she gasped. Her face was flushed, which looked better on her than it had a right to. It was easy to see why Maxwell Cullen had married Elizabeth. She was truly lovely, with high cheekbones and curly hair the color of waxed chestnuts. She was, however, difficult. Apparently, Cullen merely ignored his wife's flaws. Rather than pacifying her, he "went hunting," leaving his staff to deal with Elizabeth's frequent tantrums, which, rumor had it, including throwing china and other fragile objects. Though Elizabeth was lovely, and considerably younger than Cullen, Ravi did not envy the man.

"Can you believe that some boor from North America would accuse *me*," Elizabeth spat, "of being disloyal to my Maxwell?"

She looked up at him with her big, brown eyes and lashes like butterfly wings.

Why, yes, in fact, Ravi thought, *I can indeed.*

"I'm sure that's not what he intended to say," Ravi said. "Perhaps you are misinterpreting his words? Either way, you mustn't feel insulted. He will be departing tomorrow and you shan't see him again. It's a lovely day, don't you think?"

She laughed lightly. "Oh, you do cheer me up."

"Shall we go back to the grand staircase?" Ravi asked.

"Oh, no, not yet," Elizabeth said.

"We don't want to miss the Viceroy's arrival," Ravi said.

"But I think," Elizabeth said, fanning her chest rapidly, "I think I might swoon."

"I will get you some water," Ravi said.

"No, no, just stay," she said, holding his arm.

Oh, dear, thought Ravi.

"I should—"

Elizabeth's eyes rolled back and she fell into his arms. A thin line of sweat trickled from her neck down the front of her bodice. A few rogue curls escaped from under her hat, tumbling down the side of her flushed face. He watched her chest rising and falling.

What am I going to do? His eyes darted back and forth, seeking an avenue of escape, while occasionally landing on the undoubtedly attractive woman he now held in his arms.

"Mucker-jee!"

Ravi knew that voice, also. It was the frequently shouting voice of Maxwell Cullen. Ravi was used to the mispronunciation of his name. All the British called him Mucker-jee, or some such. Right now, that was the least of his worries.

Ravi closed his eyes. It was not going to be a good day, after all.

Cullen appeared around the corner, yelling the whole way.

"Gangly told me you cancelled my elephants. Now, why on earth would you—"

Cullen's already buggy eyes goggled even more beneath his pith helmet when he saw Elizabeth swooning in his arms.

"W-What on God's green earth is going on?" he stammered.

Elizabeth was up in a heartbeat. "Hello, darling. Ravi was kind enough to offer me some water and a fan when I was feeling ill because of the heat and the crowds. You know how the weather here gets to me," she said shakily.

"What? The weather?" Cullen was sputtering. He pointed a bony finger at Ravi. "You. I don't care if she falls to the ground like a sack of potatoes. You don't—allow a man's wife—an Englishman's wife—*my* wife—to swoon in your arms."

Ravi would not have been surprised if Cullen had started foaming at the mouth in an apoplectic fit. "Now, Major Cullen," Ravi began.

"Don't you 'Major Cullen' me," he spat. "Between this and the elephants, you are through at ICS. I don't ever want to see your face at Dalhousie square again. Be cleared out before tomorrow morning."

"But—Major Cullen!" Ravi protested.

"Not another word or I'll find a way to have you jailed. That's what we get for giving natives opportunities." Though Ravi had suspected Cullen thought this, it was still a slap in the face. "You couldn't manage a puppet show. Incompetent, the lot of you."

The second rifle salute thundered around them, signaling the Viceroy's arrival at the government house. Cullen turned, and in an undignified manner, sprinted to the front of the house.

"Oh, don't you mind Maxwell," Elizabeth began.

"Excuse me, ma'am," Ravi said absently. He turned, drifting back toward the crowd as if in a dream.

"Ravi, wait," she said, but he did not. He weaved through the crowd, careful not to jostle anyone, though he wondered if he would feel it if he did. He felt oddly like an apparition, as if he were not really there.

The new Viceroy was shaking hands with the Lieutenant Governor. Lord Curzon, much younger than his predecessor Elgin, was positively glowing. He looked at the building that was now both his official and private home, and with suitably British pomp declared that, "This is, doubtless, the finest Government House occupied by the representative of any sovereign in the world."

The crowd applauded. Ravi stood watching, until Cullen caught his eye. Cullen glowered at him, and Ravi was surprised that all the foliage around him did not immediately shrivel and die. Cullen pointed angrily toward the road.

Cullen's sour look changed into an obsequious smile as Curzon looked in his direction, but as soon as Curzon turned away, he was back to glowering at Ravi and gesturing away from the government house.

Ravi could do nothing but comply.

Chapter

Ravi woke at his usual time and set about his morning routine. Much of his gloom from the previous day had passed as he thought over exactly what had happened. He resolved to go to work as though nothing had changed, and as expected he arrived at Writers' to find things settled more or less back to normal after the previous day's festivities. While in no hurry to confirm his assumption with a face-to-face encounter, he expected to find that Cullen had forgotten about or at least thought better of firing him. It was not the first time Maxwell Cullen had become enraged and threatened to terminate, imprison, hang or otherwise be rid of an employee who caught his momentary ire and Ravi was quite certain that all would be back to comfortable normality in short order.

He found that Maxwell Cullen had in fact made a point of informing the staff to deny Ravi entry to the building. To add further to the humiliation, two sepoys were on hand to physically remove Ravi should he protest.

Ravi wandered down the steps of the Writers' Building and across Dalhousie Square, only numbly aware of the foot and horse traffic around him. Thousands of people went about their business as he trudged on aimlessly. He paid little attention to the people flitting about the square, nor did he give much thought to the English architecture that surrounded him as he turned west at the Post Office and wandered to the Strand.

Ravi sat on the grass at the edge of Eden Park, where he could think and watch the ships on the Hooghly. English merchant ships with towering sails moved like giants amidst a swarm of little native fishing boats. He watched the boats, the pedestrians, the Europeans walking by the Hindu beggars and street merchants.

"Excuse me," a voice called out. Ravi turned, seeing a stocky and unpleasant-looking white man stomping away from a motorized carriage. Ravi's attention immediately focused on the machine, with its elegantly simple transmission and engine unadorned by decorative flourishes.

"Yes, you," he said, pointing at Ravi. "Indian fellow. Might I have a word?"

The man's accent was a bit odd. He did not sound like the other Englishmen he had met, and Ravi wondered where he was from.

"Of course, sir," he said reflexively.

"Call me Hiram," he said, eyeballing Ravi. Ravi was suddenly conscious of the fact that he was the only Indian in the park wearing a tailored English suit. He was also aware that it was far more flattering than Hiram's rumpled, sweaty-marked, oil-stained tweeds. "Are you Ravi Mukherjee?"

"Yes, sir. I am," Ravi answered.

Hiram scowled, but instead of scolding him for some minor offense, Hiram produced from his pocket an old copy of the *British Journal of Engineering and the Sciences*.

Ravi's eyes widened. He knew that on page fifty-seven began a paper entitled *Dirigible Craft as an Alternative to Rail for Rural Commerce and Administration*. It had never occurred to him that someone outside the administration would take note of his proposal, particularly since he had not been able to inspire anyone within it to do so.

"This Ravi Mukherjee? I've been driving around for hours looking for you! Why in God's name aren't you at work?"

"I, ahh," Ravi stammered. "I am sorry, sir."

"Don't apologize. Explain."

"I have been dismissed, sir," Ravi replied. The words weighed on him.

Hiram smiled.

"Perfect," Hiram said, accompanied by clasping his hands together in a fist to palm clap. "I have a job that should interest you if you'd be so good as to step into my carriage." He turned to walk back to the vehicle that was still chuffing out a hazy black cloud, but stopped in mid pivot to look back at Ravi. "And stop calling me sir."

Ravi sat across from Hiram, facing him as Hiram looked past him, driving the carriage. Ravi wasn't sure what he found more disconcerting, talking to a man who looked past him as though he weren't there or not being able to see where they were going.

"Your proposal had a good deal of merit," Hiram was saying without ever looking Ravi in the eye. "A trifle naive, but reasonably well thought out. And a good understanding of the limitations of dirigibles."

"I was very young when I wrote that proposal," Ravi answered.

"You were innovative, before administration stifled that. If you still have that ability to think outside of what you are told is possible, I would like you to assist me."

"With what, if I might ask?" Ravi was finding himself intrigued by more than the mere prospect of gainful employment.

"Pushing back the frontiers of scientific knowledge," Hiram answered. With that, he spared a second's attention to look directly at Ravi. "Don't look all flustered, I don't need a proper scientist," Hiram continued. "I need a bean-counter with the ability to reason scientifically. Someone who understands just enough to not pester me with silly questions."

"I am interested in employment, sir—"

"Bloody Hell! Stop saying that," Hiram demanded.

"I don't know what else to call an Englishman," Ravi replied, genuinely uncomfortable.

Hiram squeezed the brake, bringing the carriage to a sudden halt. He glared at Ravi.

"Englishman? I am deeply insulted," Hiram said. "We haven't endured seven hundred years of English oppression to be mistaken for them by the likes of you." He turned his eyes from Ravi, let out a disgusted snort, and jerked the carriage back into gear.

"My apologies," Ravi said.

"You don't see me floundering about, mistaking you for a Zulu." He gave the carriage more throttle, jolting Ravi in his seat as the contraption lurched forward over an unpaved road out of Kolkata.

After an uncomfortable silence, Ravi asked, "if you are not from England, where, then, are you from?"

"I am from Belfast. Ireland!" said Hiram. "You've never met an Irishman?"

Ravi shook his head.

Hiram scoffed. "I suppose I can forgive you, in that event."

They rode for nearly two hours, mostly following a narrow dirt road that was barely adequate for travel. Hiram made no effort at conversation, save for periodic questions of a direct and businesslike nature aimed at clarifying details of Ravi's time with ICS. Because Ravi faced the rear of the vehicle, he rarely looked to see where they were going due to the discomfort of trying to contort himself around on the wooden bench seat within the cramped confines of the carriage. He didn't see their destination until they were approaching the gate.

A wall of vertical logs reminiscent of an Eighteenth Century fort protruded some twenty feet into the air and sprawled out into a perimeter that, as near as Ravi could estimate, enclosed perhaps a dozen acres. Ravi twisted in his seat, looking out the window behind him as they passed through the open gate. Inside the wall were several buildings, most prominently a massive structure he recognized as a dirigible hangar. Others appeared to be factories, barracks and warehouses. Indian workers scurried about in groups, hauling coal and tools and wooden crates. Ravi turned to Hiram, starting to ask questions of his own.

Ravi froze in confusion as a bolt of lightning shot past them with a loud crack and a peculiar odor he couldn't place.

"Bugger it all," Hiram grumbled as the carriage jerked to a halt. "Gunter!" he shouted in the direction from which the bolt had come.

A tall, fierce-looking blonde man was holding a rifle the likes of which Ravi had never seen. Its heavy steel barrel was nearly as thick as a man's arm and ringed at intervals of one inch or so in copper until the rear of the weapon, which was bulkier still and contained an apparatus Ravi couldn't begin to identify. The entire device was housed in a hardwood stock that, even at considerable distance, was clearly made by a skilled artisan, though not given the highest level of the craftsman's attention.

Gunter again shouldered the weapon, aimed in the general direction of the carriage, and fired. Ravi involuntarily gasped as another flash of lightning shot past the carriage and struck a sloth bear that had been digging into an ant hill, oblivious to the goings on around it.

The bear dropped to the ground, convulsing for a moment before becoming still.

"Is he all right?" a voice exclaimed. *A woman's voice*, Ravi realized, as he turned his head in her direction.

She was young, perhaps eighteen, and wore an ensemble consisting of a pith helmet, bicycle suit, long socks and a white shirt with a bow-tie carelessly askew. She batted away a honey-blonde curl which had tumbled free from the hat.

"Merely stunned," Gunter answered with an arrogant nod as he lowered the weapon from his shoulder. At that point he turned his attention to a uniformed British officer who was observing the test. "That was the Iron Wolfe's lowest setting, Major," he continued. He held the lightning gun out to the Major, who merely looked at it with a skeptical eye.

"Put that infernal thing down!" Hiram shouted as he stomped across the grounds towards them with Ravi trailing behind and nervously looking around.

"At last," Gunter bellowed with mock relief, "our luminary has returned."

Hiram paid him just enough attention to be denigrating before settling in to ignoring him completely. "Mukherjee," he began, "This is Major Westbridge and his lovely daughter Sophia." He turned to Gunter, looking him over with exaggerated contempt. "Don't you think you've wasted enough time on that contraption of yours?"

"I need something to alleviate the tedium of fabricating replacement gyroscopes," Gunter shot back.

"I can hardly take full responsibility for that fiasco," Hiram replied.

"Though it was entirely your fault," Gunter retorted. "While the Iron Wolfe is a triumph of engineering," he added with excessive pride.

"It burnt down your lab," Hiram shot back. "We all call it Wolfe's Bane," he added to Major Westbridge. "Ask him to demonstrate it in the rain sometime."

Hiram turned his attention back to Ravi as though Gunter had simply disappeared from awareness. "Come along so we can get you settled in. I want you to start work first thing tomorrow morning." Ravi followed as Hiram walked toward the factory building. "I expect that we shall be expanding our operation here in the coming weeks, once we have proven ourselves. As for Gunter, he's usually very unpleasant company and best avoided."

Gunter was eager to resume his pitch to Major Westbridge, but found himself forced to tag along as the Major and Sophia followed Hiram.

Ravi, feeling a bit overwhelmed, quietly kept pace as Hiram and Gunter found ever more creative ways to insult one another.

Not wanting to be drawn into their feud, Ravi took in the details of his new place of employment. The largest building looked comparable to any major factory in London, utilitarian and devoid of character. His clerk's mind began tallying cost estimates for the facility, which clearly had obtained considerable funding from somewhere.

What Ravi's attention to detail missed, however, was the look of disgust on some of the Indian laborers as they watched the stunned bear slowly stagger up from the ground and shake off the effects of Gunter's lightning gun.

3
Chapter

Ravi's room was small, much smaller than his apartment. However, as he had anticipated, he did not much miss his things. After he had unpacked, Hiram had knocked in order to personally extend a dinner invitation. This more than made up for the smallness of the space. Cullen would no more have invited him to dinner than he would have put on a tutu and danced a ballet.

He tentatively entered the dining room, unsure of the protocol. The room was simple but elegant, contrasting the austere factory complex and boarding house.

"Come, my good man. Sit!" said Hiram, from the head of the table. Ravi noted that Hiram had not changed clothes for dinner.

Servants were just bringing out mulligatawny soup. Ravi lifted his spoon and awkwardly stirred, hoping it wasn't obvious that he wasn't eating. He had been raised vegetarian, and had not once in his life eaten chicken or beef, not even while studying in London. After the soup came salted beef tongue and chicken tikka masala. He was beginning to wish he had been excluded from the meal after all when the servants brought out kedgeree, a simple dish consisting of fish, rice and eggs. *Oh, thank goodness*, he thought. He feared that his growling stomach was becoming audible, and he couldn't drink enough water to silence it.

Hiram's enthusiastic eating did not impair his ability to dominate the conversation. "Well there was certainly a good deal of pomp surrounding his arrival," he was saying. "You know how the English love ceremony. No offense to you or your daughter, Major Westbridge."

"None taken," replied Westbridge.

Sophia had swapped her bicycle suit for a proper dress and stylish hat. Still, her thick honey-blonde curls refused to stay neatly tucked away, and the bow tie was still lopsided.

"How will the new Viceroy affect your work here, Mister Codon?" she asked.

Hiram scoffed. "Not one whit. My work is backed by Cecil Rhodes and through him, Her Majesty Queen Victoria herself. I expect Curzon will simply ignore me, as did Elgin."

Ravi was taken aback. "Rhodes? From the British South Africa company? What has he to do with India?"

"Absolutely nothing," Hiram said. He smiled smugly, shoving a large forkful of the chicken into his mouth.

Gunter Wolfe, who had eaten little and said even less, stated, "The source of funds has nothing to do with where we operate. Europe is too far north—"

"And equatorial Africa is not suited to industry of any kind," Hiram interrupted.

"And Rhodes' insistence on the territory being British, despite considerable German backing for this project," Gunter grumbled.

Hiram leaned forward to Ravi and whispered loudly, in a mock conspiratorial fashion, "Gunter keeps promising support from the Kaiser, but I have yet to see a single Mark."

Gunter glowered. "That is the fault of your government, not mine."

Ravi cleared his throat. "What exactly is it that you intend to accomplish?"

Gunter opened his mouth to speak, but Hiram interrupted, again. "Some things are better shown rather than told, my dear Mister Mukherjee. This is a dinner party. Eat!"

"So I'm not the only one left in the dark," Sophia said, with a sidelong glance at her father.

Westbridge sighed deeply. "Sophia, how many times must I tell you? There is simply no place for women in the sciences."

"That's not true, there's a woman physicist at the Sorbonne," said Sophia.

"Poppycock," Westbridge replied through a spoonful of pudding.

"It's true, father."

Ravi smiled. "You are speaking of Madame Curie, then, Miss Westbridge?"

"Mister Mukherjee, you've heard of her!"

Surprised, Ravi glanced at Sophia.

"Why, you look shocked," she said.

"You pronounced my name correctly, miss, that is all."

Sophia laughed, a light sound like the tinkling of bells. "Well, it isn't brain surgery," she said. "Mister Codon, you said he was a bureaucrat."

"I was a bureaucrat, miss," said Ravi. "It's true. But I have some small scientific curiosity."

"Ah, Mister Mukherjee is being modest. He's actually been published," said Hiram. Gunter glanced up from his plate, re-appraising Ravi. Though his look contained his typical disdain, it was the first time he seemed to regard Ravi at all.

"Oh?" he said.

Sophia looked delighted. "I'd love to read your papers."

Ravi felt himself flush. Though flattered, he remembered the response he had gotten from ICS, and didn't relish the thought of Sophia's disrespect. *Though she seems to value innovation*, he thought, *unlike Maxwell Cullen*.

"I just had my fourth paper published by the British Royal Society," said Gunter.

"Yes, Doctor Wolfe," said Sophia, "that's the fourth time you've mentioned that today."

Gunter gave Sophia a cold look, but with something underneath. Hurt? *He very much wants to impress Sophia,* Ravi realized.

Though Ravi was a master at keeping a neutral expression, Gunter lashed out at him, anyway. "Some small scientific curiosity is one thing. Our work is quite complex, and not for the average lay person. If I were you, I would stick to keeping the books."

"Yes, yes, and me to managing the household. How tedious," Sophia said, tossing back the rest of her wine in a very unladylike fashion.

"Tosh! Sophia, don't be rude," said Westbridge.

Though the argument between Westbridge and his daughter seemed habitual, as did the competitiveness between Gunter and Hiram, Ravi was still embarrassed. In attempt to diffuse the tension, he said, "Are you also interested in the sciences Major Westbridge?"

"I am here strictly in a military capacity," he said.

Hiram winked at Ravi, and said in his exaggerated whisper, "Major Westbridge is my minder, so to speak. He's here to make sure I'm not wasting the Crown's money."

"And quite a lot of money it is, don't you forget," said Westbridge.

Hiram laughed. "And how could I, Major, with you here to remind me?"

"If I may ask…"

"In time. Now it's time to eat, not work."

Sophia glanced at Ravi, and then rolled her eyes as if commiserating.

****

The night shift on the factory floor consisted of a skeleton crew. A handful of workers were staffing posts or carrying materials across the catwalks.

Javesh Ram, distracted, half-heartedly dropped a glass object, bottle-shaped with a round end, in a crate. He winced at the sound of shattered glass. He reached into the container, finding that he had shattered two. They would both need to be re-blown. He sighed heavily.

Another worker stopped, calling to Javesh in Hindi. "What's wrong with you? I can't finish this by myself."

Javesh gave him a long, hard look. "I'm not sure we should finish it at all."

"Oh please," the other man scoffed. "You're not going to tell me about the sloth bear again, are you?"

"An arc of lightning!" cried Javesh. "The tube threw lighting and it dropped that bear in an instant. And the white man just looked at the bear like it was nothing. What if that bear was you? What if it was your children?"

Other workers stopped what they were doing, some muttering in assent, some in annoyance.

"Don't be stupid. You're very paranoid."

"You short sighted fool! Maybe it isn't now, but it might be, sooner than you think."

A few of the workers nodded at this.

"He's right, I saw. That Doctor Wolfe is a frightening man," one said.

"Oh, shut up, the lot of you," another said. "I want to go home before sunrise."

Whatever their opinions were, most of the workers had stopped what they were doing and were listening.

"Even if you are right, what do you suggest we do about it?" the other said. "My family was begging in the streets until I got this job. I need this job."

On another day, Javesh may have fallen silent. He did not usually think of himself as a rebel. But now he had an audience. Some of the workers seemed to be agreeing with him, and they were looking to see what he would say next. "It's their fault you were starving to begin with! We should go back to our own ways, not build weapons for them to kill us! Doesn't anyone here remember eighteen-fifty-seven? If you don't, then think of your fathers," he cried.

Even as he said it, it felt a little like posturing. Javesh had not yet been born, and his father had barely been involved. Still, even though the attempted revolution had failed, it was widespread enough to roust the East India Company. It had been replaced, unfortunately, not by self-rule, but by direct rule by the British Queen Victoria.

The other worker seemed taken aback. "No one is killing anyone," he said softly. "Codon has been good to the workers. The famine has not touched us."

Spooked from the lightening gun, frustrated from breaking the glass objects, and now angry at being dismissed by his fellow workers, Javesh picked up the entire crate and hurled it into the wall. Glass shards rained down on the floor. "They can't kill us if we destroy their weapons."

Other workers took Javesh's lead, smashing fragile components.

"Wait! Stop! You're jumping to conclusions! We don't even know what they are building."

Someone, not Javesh, threw a vacuum tube at his friend, who took cover behind a stack of crates.

"Exactly," Javesh said. "Why doesn't that scare you?"

Someone threw a tube at Javesh. Before he knew what was happening, a brawl had broken out on the factory floor.

****

Ravi watched Sophia eat the last bite of her generous portion of apple tart. She had easily eaten as much as any of the men, Hiram included, and he wondered where the slip of a girl put it all.

Her father was also watching, but with something like disapproval. "This is when ladies usually retire, Sophia," he said.

"So it is," she said, her eyes sparkling. She made no move to get up from the table.

"Perhaps we should all retire," Hiram said with a barely disguised yawn. "We do have an early day, tomorrow."

"About that, sir," Ravi said. Before Hiram could protest, he amended, "That is, Mister Codon. What exactly will I be doing?"

"We've got about sixty workers in three shifts. I need you to manage them, make sure they meet our production timetables."

Gunter scoffed.

"What's rattling around inside your skull, Gunter?" Hiram demanded.

"What's rattling around is your workers," Gunter said snidely.

"Nonsense, you egotistical Hun, those men are the best workforce I could ask for. They are dedicated and efficient."

"They're discontent."

"My workers are not discontent."

A crash came from the factory floor, followed by an outcry. Gunter smirked, raising his glass to Hiram.

Westbridge rose, followed by Hiram, Ravi and Sophia.

When they entered the factory, they found that the whole floor had erupted into a riot. Smashed glass littered the floor, and one of the windows was even broken.

Westbridge ran in to break up the fight, with Ravi and Hiram close behind. Ravi pulled Javesh and the other worker apart.

Javesh glared at Ravi. "What is wrong with you, you British lapdog?" he yelled in Hindi. "How can you work for these evil men?"

"I see you are employed in the same factory as I am," Ravi said wryly.

"Who is responsible for this?" shouted Hiram.

The worker who had been fighting with Javesh pointed. "That one," he said.

Hiram turned to another worker. "Is this true?" he asked.

The other worker nodded.

Hiram glared at Javesh. "You!" he said. "Don't come back. The rest of you, go home. The job will still be here tomorrow, if you want it."

The workers filed out, some grumbling, some chagrined.

As they left, Gunter elbowed his way through. "Yes, yes, very content. I'm sure your Queen would applaud your use of her treasury."

4

Chapter

Not for the first time that morning, Ravi's forehead hit the desk, which was not as nice as his mahogany desk at home. Neither was it as nice as his desk at ICS. In fact, the office space was downright shabby—small, cramped and loud. The noise was understandable, since his office overlooked the factory floor. This location also accounted for the chemical smell, which made Ravi lightheaded. His breakfast shifted in his stomach. The one small window which looked out on the grounds was already open all the way, so he would just have to hope he got used to it.

My life will never be the same, he says, Ravi thought irritably. *Never the same as what, I wonder.*

Though Hiram had only fired the instigator of last night's riot, several others had not shown up for work this morning. Ravi assumed they would not be back. The roster was very short, in fact, and he had not been given adequate information about the remaining workers. While some of the stations were manned by unskilled laborers, others required certain training or skills.

Without knowing who was who, Ravi was finding it difficult to organize the work detail. Ravi couldn't imagine why Hiram would hire an administrator only to hide all the relevant information from him.

Englishmen, Ravi thought irritably. *Assign you a task and provide no tools with which to complete it. Oh, but he's Irish*, he reminded himself. *Rubbish.*

Ravi looked onto the factory floor in time to see Gunter storming up the stairs. The German scientist unceremoniously threw open the door to Ravi's office and smacked down a stack of papers. Ravi stood, refusing to be intimidated.

"I need these five men re-assigned to me, immediately," said Gunter, glowering.

Ravi glanced down at the list, and then made eye contact with Gunter.

"I'm sorry? I did not see that they had assignments. They appeared to be reserve," he said calmly, as if Gunter had made his request in a reasonable manner. Ravi was reminded of Maxwell Cullen when he was in one of his moods. Ravi had become somewhat adept at dealing with it. *Not adept enough*, he thought wryly.

Gunter gave Ravi an unpleasant smile. "Appeared to be? This is very complex, technical work that appears to be quite mystifying to the untrained eye. There is a reason for every assignment on that roster. Frankly, I don't understand why you are here at all."

Ravi didn't break eye contact. "I am here at Mister Codon's request. To organize the work detail."

"Do not make decisions based on your limited understanding. If you are not told specifically to do something, leave it alone," Gunter growled.

"Perhaps I would be of better service if someone would give me the details," said Ravi.

Gunter scoffed. "You don't need the details."

"If the workers know about your sensitive experiments, surely you can tell me," Ravi said, increasingly frustrated.

"How would you assume they know? They just do what they are told. As should you," spat Gunter.

Ravi bristled. "If you'll excuse me, sir, I report to Mister Codon. Not to you."

Gunter leaned in close to Ravi. Though Ravi was tall for an Indian man, Gunter was tall for a European. When he drew himself to his full height, he was able to successfully loom.

"If I were in your position," Gunter said, "I would stay on our good side."

"Our?" Ravi asked, though Gunter's subtle German accent made his meaning all too clear.

"There are things afoot you are not remotely aware of, and I assure you that you do not want to make an enemy of me." Gunter gave him a look that Ravi knew was intended to be sinister. Ravi wanted to laugh, but stifled it. While not intimidated by Gunter, he was, in fact, concerned. He honestly had no idea what was going on here, or what Gunter was capable of. Should he mention this to Hiram? Surely Hiram knew about the character of his partner. What about Hiram's character? Were they in agreement?

"I want those men back by noon," said Gunter, and stalked out.

Ravi glanced down at the work detail. His forehead hit the desk again.

Maybe he needed to stretch his legs. He stood, rubbing his eyes, and went over to the little window. Sophia was crossing the grounds. She was back to wearing the bicycle suit and pith helmet. The quirky style somehow looked good on her, with her suntanned face, unruly hair and the light dusting of freckles across her nose. Ravi knew she was not the type to be considered beautiful by the English, unlike Elizabeth Cullen, but he found Sophia vastly more interesting.

You're doing it again, an inner voice chided. *What is it with you and your bosses' wives and daughters? She's not Hiram's daughter*, he told the voice. *A minor detail*, said the first voice. *A military officer's daughter is probably even worse.*

She crossed the grounds with a determined gait. Gunter, leaving the factory, intercepted her. Ravi crossed his arms. *What is the man up to, now?* He wondered.

At first Sophia kept walking. Gunter reached for her arm. Then she stopped, turning toward him, eyes flashing. She said something, and he responded, but Ravi was too far away to hear. Gunter started to adjust her bow tie as if she were a child. She angrily turned away, but he held her arm fast. Her voice rose, as did Gunter's. When Gunter grabbed Sophia's other arm, Ravi turned. He was going to put a stop to this. It was one thing to attempt to intimidate another man, but manhandling a lady, even an adventurous and not entirely ladylike lady, was another matter.

By the time he got outside, however, Gunter was storming off in the other direction, presumably toward his workshop. Ravi heard a door click, and turned. That must have been Sophia, disappearing through the factory's back door, into the restricted area.

Ravi peered around to see if anyone was watching. He moved over to the door and reached for the knob, but it didn't turn. He pulled on it anyway, but it had locked behind her. Frustrated, he crept along the back wall, peering into cloudy windows that did not reveal what was beyond them. The next door he came upon was the loading dock. He nodded to a worker, who seemed surprised to see him. Not wanting to seem suspicious, he walked into the building and onto the factory floor.

The chemical smell was more pronounced on this side of the building. Ravi stopped breathing through his nose, wondering what was seeping into his lungs. Other than the industrial odors, though, the environment here was more like a collection of unrelated workshops than a single factory complex. In one corner, a blacksmith hammered away on steel, shaping it into something Ravi couldn't identify. At another station, a jeweler was working on an array of tiny metal pieces. *How odd,* he mused.

At another, a glass blower was making equally strange objects. Ravi picked one up and peered at it. It looked like a straight bottle with a round bottom. The blower set another one down to cool. Ravi noticed a crate full of these objects. He thought this was where Javesh Ram, the one who had started the riot, had been working.

"Excuse me," Ravi said.

"Yes, sir?" the worker said politely, but with a mistrustful look.

"What are these for?"

The worker looked at him blankly. "You don't know?" he asked. Ravi merely raised his eyebrows and waited for a response.

The worker shrugged. "I was given a drawing and asked to keep making these objects until told to stop."

"Asked by whom?"

"Why, Mister Codon, of course."

Ravi found that he felt relieved. He had feared the man would say Doctor Wolfe.

"And you don't know what they will be used for?" Ravi asked.

The worker shook his head.

"Is this where Javesh Ram works?" Ravi asked.

"I believe so, but we do not work the same shift," said the worker.

"Has he said anything to you about the incident last night?"

The worker looked reluctant to answer. Finally, he said, "no, but I heard. I will say that he doesn't speak for all of us."

"That's good to know," Ravi said. He moved on.

He stopped as he passed a massive coal-fired boiler, which seemed to be connected to a huge brass-bodied boiler above. Pipes joined it to six turbines, all spinning madly as the pressurized steam flowed. The turbines, in turn, were connected to thick copper wire.

There's no linkage, thought Ravi. *What does it run?*

His eyes drifted back toward the restricted area, and he thought he saw a female silhouette moving across one of the windows. He headed toward it. As he approached the back of the building, a hand clapped his shoulder. Startled, Ravi wheeled, expecting to see Wolfe, again.

"Are you lost m'boy?" asked Hiram, jovially.

"No s-Mister Codon. I am trying to find out workers' levels of expertise. There have been some issues manning the stations, with the reduction in personnel. And Doctor Wolfe has been very insistent demanding that certain workers be reserved for him."

At this, Hiram leaned back on his heels. "Oh, he has, has he? Well, when he can pay the workers, he can assign them to his own pet projects. Put the workers where they are needed. Leave the good doctor to me."

Ravi nodded. "But about the workers' backgrounds—"

"You are doing a fine job, Mister Mukherjee. Carry on."

Off he went, with his lumbering, vaguely pachyderm-like gait.

"Infuriating," huffed a voice behind him. Ravi whirled for the second time in as many minutes.

"Miss Westbridge," Ravi sighed.

"In the flesh," she said, amused, "though you look as if you'd seen a ghost."

"You startled me."

"I can see I had," her eyes sparkled. "Yes, it is loud in here, so you can't hear people approaching from behind."

"You were saying?" he asked.

"I was saying that my father and Mister Codon are infuriating. They hire you to do a job, and refuse to give you the information you need to do it."

"Those were my thoughts, also," Ravi said.

"Well, I plan to find out what is going on around here, whether they like it or not. Uh, oh. Gunter's back." She ducked behind one of the work stations as he passed a window. "I'd better go. Will I see you for tea?" she asked, but before he could answer, she ducked onto the loading dock.

Ravi saw Wolfe's silhouette passing into the restricted area.

Chapter 5

For the next several days, Ravi had little time to investigate. Trying to keep the factory running with only a skeleton crew was proving to be more of a challenge than he'd thought. And he was having a hard time reconciling the ledgers. There were some things that didn't add up, things that made no apparent sense. He peered at a receipt for a one-thousand, two-hundred yard shipment of silk.

Frustrated, he marched down the precarious metal stairs onto the factory floor. He approached the young foreman, Sanjay, who was manning Javesh Ram's station. Ravi thrust the receipt under his nose.

"What on earth does Codon need all this silk for?" he demanded.

Sanjay, taken aback, shrugged. "If I spent my time trying to figure out why Mister Codon does things, I'd never have time to work," he said simply.

Ravi sighed heavily.

"There were several seamstresses here, too. For weeks," the foreman added. "Gone, now. They left right before you came."

"More questions," muttered Ravi. Seeing the foreman's expression, he added, "Thank you. In the absence of answers, more questions will have to do. Have you noticed anything else odd?"

At this, Sanjay laughed. "Everything that happens around here is odd, I'm afraid. Can you be more specific?"

Out of the corner of his eye, Ravi saw movement. He turned toward the window. He was certain he'd seen a face peering in at them from outside, but his eyes could have been playing tricks. The windows were all coated in a thin layer of grime, and he wouldn't have been able to hear anyone rustling around outside above all the noise. Oh, well. It probably didn't matter. The person outside could probably not see Ravi any better than Ravi could see him.

He glanced toward the back of the factory. A female silhouette moved past a window.

"If you'll excuse me," Ravi said. Since he could hardly be inconspicuous, he walked toward the restricted area as if he had the authority to be there. When he found the door unsurprisingly locked, he made a show of patting down his jacket for keys that didn't exist, shaking his head and heading back toward his office. As he did so, he peeked through the cloudy windows into the back room. It was definitely Sophia. When she glanced up, he stepped out of view, but not before he saw her ducking, also. Had she seen him?

When no one was looking, he left the floor and walked around the building to the back entrance. He tried the knob. It didn't turn, but Ravi noticed it wasn't latched. He tugged, and the door opened, noiselessly. He slipped through.

He slunk through a dusty hallway to a door marked "Hiram Codon," which was partially open. He poked his head in and peered about the small office. No one appeared to be in here.

On the desk were a stack of papers, which looked like they had been shuffled through. He reached for them, then pulled his hand back. This was unethical, was it not? Then he thought of Doctor Wolfe and his lightning gun and the workers' riot.

Ravi leafed through the papers. On the top of the stack was a receipt for three and a quarter tons of bauxite. His brow furrowed in concentration.

He heard movement in the hallway, and ducked behind the desk. From underneath, he saw Sophia's low shoes, stockings, and the bottom part of her bicycling pants as she snuck across the room. She reached onto the desk and began to shuffle through the same stack of papers Ravi had been shuffling through a few seconds ago.

Voices on the factory floor grew louder, moving in their direction. Ravi, already down, stayed still. Sophia, apparently afraid someone would see her through the window, dropped to the floor.

They came nose to nose under the desk.

"Miss Westbridge," Ravi whispered. "Are you snooping?"

Her eyes widened. "So are you!" she said.

Ravi shushed her. She dropped her voice to a whisper. "Unless you care to deny it. I suppose you are huddling here under Hiram's desk waiting for a cyclone to hit."

Ravi thought about trying to come up with a plausible story, but merely shrugged. "What have you found?" he whispered.

Sophia peeked above the desk to see if the coast was clear, and then stood.

"Look at what I found in Gunter's office," Sophia said, handing him a stack of papers.

"How did you get in Doctor Wolfe's office?"

"I borrowed his keys," she said. Ravi raised an eyebrow at her. "Without his knowledge," she added. "Believe me, it wasn't easy. He's a lot more suspicious than Hiram. I think he suspects, but he can't prove anything."

Ravi looked at the letter. It was addressed to Doktor Gunter Wolfe and signed by Heinrich Goering, Governor of Namibia.

"Can you read German?" he asked.

She shook her head. "Not much. I was hoping you could."

Ravi scanned it, a single word catching his eye. "Kryolith," he said.

"Cold stone?" Sophia asked.

"Cryolite," Ravi said. "And there's a receipt here for a large shipment of bauxite. It's my understanding that aluminum metal can be refined from these minerals using electrolysis. Which would explain—"

"Those enormous boilers," Sophia said. "Yes, I thought they were for electricity, but didn't see—"

"What they were being used to power," Ravi finished. He pulled a sketch pad out of his jacket pocket and began to draw.

"What if—? You know, a rigid airship with an aluminum frame would be much lighter than wood and steel," he said.

He continued to scribble as he spoke. "They could make the ships bigger. Enormous, even. Increased cargo capacity, more passengers."

Ravi looked up, as if he were actually seeing a gargantuan aluminum-framed airship flying overhead. "Something like this could revolutionize travel. Especially with Codon's wireless. Imagine it, Miss Westbridge. This is brilliant!"

Sophia laughed, like wind chimes.

Ravi looked at her questioningly.

"Assuming that's what they are doing. Maybe you just thought of that, just now," she said.

"Perhaps," he said. "I wonder what they were doing with all that silk."

"I can't imagine! Do you think they could make it even lighter with an aluminum frame and silk stretched over it? I wondered if they were doing something with wings or sails, but couldn't figure out how it made sense."

Ravi continued to sketch. "Something like this just might work. Brilliant, Miss Westbridge!"

She laughed again. "You keep thinking of all these things and then deciding you are figuring out what other people have already thought of. Look at this," she said; gesturing to Ravi's sketch of the aluminum-framed airship covered in silk, "It's entirely new. I don't think Hiram would have thought of this. And I definitely don't see Gunter coming up with it."

Sophia handed Ravi something that looked vaguely like a big steel champagne flute, roughly the size of her hand. Ravi inspected it. The strange object had threaded holes along its base, as if pipes had been connected to it. It was discolored and slightly burned on the edges.

"What is it?" Ravi asked.

Sophia shrugged. "Why don't you tell me? If you don't guess what they are actually doing with it, you'll probably come up with something better."

Ravi shook his head. "As complimentary as that is, Miss Westbridge, it really brings us no closer to a solution."

He turned back to the stack of documents from Gunter's office. Behind the letter were a series of conceptual sketches and preliminary engineering drawings.

"What's that?" Sophia said. "I didn't look while I was in there. I wanted to get out of Gunter's office."

Ravi nodded. "It looks like the blueprints for that lightning gun he demonstrated," he said. Then he looked more closely.

This design was for something similar to the Iron Wolfe, but much larger, with a longer range. It looked to be light, though, made with aluminum and other light materials. He squinted at it.

"Oh, no," he said. The blueprint was for a mounted cannon.

Alarmed, he turned to Sophia, who held up one finger. Voices were approaching. Not on the factory floor this time, but in the restricted area.

"Quick," Sophia whispered. "Into the storeroom."

They hid. Two sets of footsteps were headed their way, one lumbering, one stalking. *Hiram and Gunter*, Ravi guessed.

"You really have to stop misplacing your keys, Gunter," Hiram said.

"I didn't say I'd misplaced them," Gunter said irritably. "I said they'd gone missing."

"Don't be ridiculous," Hiram said. "Who on earth would even be interested enough to steal them?"

"Westbridge's overly curious daughter, for one," Gunter said.

"Major Westbridge has keys to this entire complex, since he is here to represent the Crown's financial interests. And those would be a lot more accessible to her than yours."

"Perhaps, but he does not have my office key."

"Sophia may be curious, but I doubt she has the interest or the patience to go through all your dry correspondence."

"I am in possession of some very sensitive, classified documents. I do not appreciate your cavalier attitude toward them."

"Well, why don't you give them to me, and I will personally assure you that no one will look at them."

"I have my reasons," said Gunter.

"Why, are you keeping secrets from me in my own complex, Gunter?" asked Hiram, with an exaggerated sense of shock.

"I have a right to work on side projects."

"Only so long as you keep your side projects, and the funding for them, apart from our primary venture. I hope I am making myself clear," Hiram said.

"The primary venture comes first, of course," Gunter said wryly.

"Very well, unless you need me to unlock anything else for you, I'm going back to my work," Hiram replied.

Ravi and Sophia huddled uncomfortably in the store room. Gunter's stalking footsteps advanced, then retreated, then came closer again. The light in the store room came on. Ravi felt rather than heard Sophia's gasp.

"Sophia, dear, you can come out, now. The rhino is gone," Gunter said pleasantly, but with an air of menace. "That is, unless you are waiting for me to pull you up by your ears like a jackrabbit."

Chapter 6

Ravi and Sophia held their breath. Ravi peeked out from under a crate, seeing only Gunter's shoes. He watched helplessly as they began to cross the room.

Gunter's feet stopped. Sophia held her breath.

"If my work fascinates you so," Gunter said in an entirely unconvincing tone of sincere friendship, "ask me to show you around. Snooping is dangerous."

She glanced at Ravi, still not breathing, desperately trying to keep silent.

"Your father would be so disappointed if you hurt yourself."

"Doctor?" the welcome voice of Major Westbridge said from the doorway. "To whom are you speaking?"

"Musing aloud," Gunter answered. "What do you want, Major?"

"I have some technical questions I would like to discuss with Mister Codon and yourself. Will you accompany me to his office?"

A barely perceptible grimace crossed Gunter's face before he nodded. "Yes. Of course."

As they left, Sophia and Ravi both exhaled in relief. While unnoticed by Ravi, Sophia caught a glimpse of her father's eyes as he glanced directly at her, peering from her hiding place. His disapproving scowl made it quite clear that he had seen her and what he thought of her sneaking about. She made a point to thank him for rescuing her when next they spoke.

Wordlessly, Ravi and Sophia replaced the papers and escaped through the back door.

****

Ravi was distracted for the remainder of the day. His conscience gnawed at him all through dinner, and now he found that he could not sleep. Tossing and turning, he was painfully aware of the insect chorus outside his window and the humming of electrical wires overhead. The blending of natural and mechanical noise was eerie to him, like an army of mechanical roaches.

He rose, ambling to the window. The rolling hills were blanketed in the indigo night sky and a thin layer of fog.

He pulled out his sketch pad and drew a set of skeletal aluminum wings with silk stretched over them. He squinted at it.

Ravi tapped his pencil, deep in thought. He then drew a kerosene engine behind and a propeller in front. Could this be what they were working on? Heavier-than-air travel? That was the holy grail of aeronauts. If Codon had figured out how such a thing could work...

And what about Wolfe's lightning cannon? Ravi paced from one corner to the other of the small room. He didn't care for the implications.

Finally, at nearly three o'clock in the morning, he laid back down. He did not think he would be able to sleep, and at first, he tossed and turned. Then he found himself fading in and out of consciousness, until he was engulfed in the heavy syrup of sleep.

A boy of thirteen, he was at the Crystal Palace in London. Nearly a million square feet, the great exhibition hall was spectacular, made of cast-iron and glass, and crowded with spectators. It was the most impressive thing he had ever seen.

In the middle of it all was a modest monoplane with a 15-foot wingspan. Two large, fan-shaped propellers were connected to a steam engine. The nondescript inventor Thomas Moy powered up the machine, which took off down the track, gaining speed.

Ravi gasped, crying out with the crowd as the front wheel pushed into the air. The craft lifted, for one second, two--then toppled over like a tired old dog. The crowd's sense of wonder dissolved into disappointed murmuring.

The scene changed. Suddenly, the aerial steamer was charging straight at him, larger than life, faster than a freight train. Ravi dove out of the way just in time.

He rolled over onto his back, staring at the sky. He was in the Indian countryside, framed by hills, dotted by trees. Thomas Moy's aerial steamer chugged away overhead. Then it morphed into the bat-like aluminum machine from his drawing. Ravi watched it, awestruck.

Then it was joined by several more. Soon, they were like locusts, filling the sky with a cloud of grey and noise. They cast a shadow over the sun. Thirteen-year-old Ravi looked into the air, and twenty-eight-year-old Ravi stood next to him, looking down at his younger self.

The shadows moved over young Ravi's face, making him look like a bizarre sideshow, some sort of illustrated man. Young Ravi seemed not to be affected by the changing scene. He stared thoughtfully into the sky just like he had a few moments ago.

Older Ravi wached helplessly as the strange aircraft, now with twin Maxim guns mounted to either side, began firing at other aircraft. Some of the planes were adorned with the Union Jack, some with the Iron Cross.

Stop, stop, stop, he tried to yell, but his voice would not work. The planes peppered the ground around him with bullets.

The grey around them deepened as the sun was entirely obscured. Ravi peered up into the turbulent sky. The planes flew toward a massive aluminum airship, bristling with Iron Wolfe cannons and raining bombs. More armed aircraft were slung to the sides on hooks, releasing and flying off like angry hornets.

Ravi's gaze followed the arc of their fire. The city below was ablaze and ruined. Desperately, he turned back to his young self, to tell him to run, but instead of his younger self, he saw an enormous clockwork lion, who reared back and pounced at him, roaring with a human voice, his voice...

Ravi jerked awake. Of course that was what they were building. It was what they always built. Well, he may not be able to stop them, but at the very least he could refuse to be a part of it.

He leapt out of bed and, in a flurry, threw the sum total of his belongings in his small suitcase. Twenty minutes later he was back in the same position he had been an hour ago, pensive and unable to sleep.

Flustered, he threw back the blankets and stomped over to his desk. He lit a candle and half-heartedly paged through a book, waiting for morning. He would turn in his resignation immediately.

Then what? He asked himself. *Oh, shut it*, he answered.

A mechanical roar tore through the air, rattling the walls. Ravi jolted upright, knocking the candle over. He frantically patted it out before the fire could catch. The infernal racket ceased, and then started again, louder this time. Ravi winced. It was like a small wrecking crew trying to break through his eardrum with a battering ram.

Confused, frightened, but intensely curious, he threw his tweed suit coat over his nightshirt and ventured outside to investigate.

The tone of the roar changed slightly to a higher octave, growing louder in the process. It sounded like an explosion that never stopped or cannons firing so rapidly that the detonations blurred together.

Now outside, Ravi could see the flicker of intense fire inside the large factory building. Some way off, he saw two of the workers running toward the factory. Instinct took over and he ran to assist. The nearest door was unlocked. "Hello," he shouted, barely able to hear his own voice over the roar.

Inside, the floor was dug nearly twenty yards down into the ground. Ravi found himself standing on a catwalk overlooking a pit. He could only see the opposite wall from the doorway, an expanse of tangled pipes and tanks wound around each other like entrails.

The roar stopped. The fire was instantly extinguished. Ravi froze in place as the building was filled with a mechanical whining that slowly dropped in pitch and volume.

A tap on his shoulder made him gasp like a startled child as he spun around to look.

Sophia stifled a laugh.

"The noise provides wonderful cover, don't you think?" she said, eyes sparkling.

"Whatever are you doing at this hour, Miss Westbridge?" Ravi asked with more impatience than he meant. Already irritable, he felt foolish for being startled yet again. "You should not be here."

"You shouldn't be here either," Sophia said even as Ravi motioned her to silence. The machine's whine cut out in the middle of her sentence, the last words hanging in the air. They both stopped, listening.

After a few moments, Ravi continued in a whisper. "This could be dangerous and—"

"Interesting," Sophia finished, grinning. "I think I saw someone breaking in. Duty requires that we investigate."

She went tramping off into the building. Ravi followed.

The catwalk led into the main structure, where it overlooked a large assembly area. The walls sloped down to form a stonework basin, half underground, as if to contain an enormous fire. A long metal cylindrical frame lay on its side, filling the space like the room was made for it.

Ravi stared at the machinery. Bulbous tanks and a maze of pipes filled the space inside the bright silvery skeleton, ending in a bell-shaped nozzle at one end. And Ravi suddenly knew. A rocket! He was staring at a rocket unlike any that had ever been constructed before.

He ducked, noticing Hiram and Westbridge walking out from behind a shielded alcove.

"The replacement gyro was installed this morning," Hiram was saying confidently. "And the coolant issue is merely a question of flow rates. We will be ready to go in a matter of days."

"And production figures if the project is funded thereafter?"

"Two every six months to start," Hiram answered, nodding his head. "Perhaps more as our production methods improve."

At a sudden insistent poking at his shoulder, Ravi turned to Sophia who pointed across the building to the opposite catwalk with her other hand.

Javesh, the factory worker behind the previous day's mutiny, was skulking around in the shadows. He had a canvas bag slung over his shoulder, held close to him.

Sophia's eyes went wide. She stood and pointed.

"Stop him!" Sophia shouted. "Dynamite!" she added as she vigorously pointed. All eyes turned to her and Ravi.

Javesh hesitated, looking to both available avenues of escape as Westbridge drew his pistol.

"No," Hiram hissed, grabbing the revolver. "Don't shoot anything in here."

Determining Ravi and Sophia to be the lesser threat, Javesh charged at them in a desperate escape attempt.

Ravi tackled him before he could plow into Sophia. Javesh tumbled face-first onto the metal catwalk, spilling a dozen sticks of dynamite from his bag in the process. Before Ravi could recover,

Javesh kicked him in the gut, knocking the wind out of him. Ravi tried fighting back even as he gasped for breath.

Javesh tried to stand. One leg was tangled in Ravi's gangly limbs. His nose and lip were bleeding profusely from the impact with the iron catwalk. His eyes were blurred from dirt and blood while Ravi tried to knock him back down.

Javesh jarred his leg free, but slipped on the blood-coated metal.

"No!" Hiram shouted as Javesh tumbled off the side.

Time seemed to slow for Ravi as he turned his head, following Javesh as he fell.

Javesh landed on a round copper-colored vat inside the rocket. Ravi expected him to roll off, painfully impacting on the metal supports before hitting the cement floor. But the tank rippled. It looked almost liquid for a moment as it flexed under the man's weight.

Then it burst like a balloon. Paper-thin walls popped under him and the contents of the vat rushed out in all directions, tendrils and drops of a liquid that Ravi would have mistaken for water if not for the horrifying fact that it dissolved Javesh's body on contact.

He was only vaguely aware of Sophia's scream. He didn't see the thin stream of the liquid that sprayed across Major Westbridge's arm, severing it cleanly just below the elbow.

A long string of curses erupted from Hiram as he applied water to Westbridge's arm.

Ravi heard yelling from outside, and saw a group of workers, who had been peering through the window, run away.

Ravi stood, horrified, staring at the pool of blood on the factory floor.

"Help me get him to the carriage," Hiram shouted to Sophia. "Mukherjee, inform the physician we need him immediately."

The scene took on a dreamlike quality. Ravi turned from the floor, to Westbridge, to Hiram.

"What in the name of all creation was that?" he yelled. His voice, usually so calm and collected, was hoarse, loud and panicked.

"The physician, Ravi. Now!"

It was only the sight of blood pooling on the catwalk from what had been Westbridge's arm that brought him back. Truly, nothing could be done for Javesh.

Ravi ran.

Chapter

Ravi woke the physician, whose expert medical advice was to prepare a carriage while he applied bandages. He stayed until Hiram arrived and gruffly dismissed him, telling him to wait in his office. He would have left then and there, where it not for the fact that the only carriage in the complex was needed to take Major Westbridge to a proper hospital, a several hour ride.

Expecting a long morning ahead followed by a longer ride back to the city, Ravi went to his room and changed into more dignified attire. Certain he would not be returning, he picked up his small suitcase and left the door open behind him.

And so Ravi found himself in Hiram's office, poking through his belongings as he waited for the inevitable admonishment followed by unemployment. Less than an hour before, he would have almost gleefully indulged his curiosity, but now his investigating was half-hearted and each intellectually thrilling discovery marred by guilt over the circumstances of his learning them.

Still, he couldn't sit in the corner like a scolded schoolboy. He read Hiram's notes and calculations that described in precise detail the launching of his previous rockets in high parabolic arcs, one landing as far as one hundred and forty miles out to sea in the Bay of Bengal. Hiram's hastily scribbled note on the military applications did not escape his notice. Ravi shuddered under visions of hundreds of rockets raining down on cities, each filled with explosives, destroying entire nations without so much as a single rifleman going in harm's way.

And yet Hiram wrote of more than thrust to weight ratios, suborbital trajectories and point of impact calculations. He had notebooks filled with speculations both mathematical and whimsical on the nature of the aether, the surface of the other planets, the composition of the stars.

And yet, as a weapon—

"Mukherjee," the ever gruff voice barked. "This not a library. Sit down."

"I would prefer to stand, Mister Codon."

"Bloody insufferable contrarian," Hiram muttered before grabbing a leather-bound notebook from a compartment under his desk. "There are four people in the world who have seen what I'm going to show you—"

"I am not certain that I want to know any more than I have already seen."

"Nonsense," Hiram almost laughed. "You want to know every buggering detail even if it horrifies you. If you'd sit down and listen instead of nosing into things, maybe you'll learn something and be pleasantly surprised. Can you do that, Mukherjee?"

Ravi's eyes narrowed. Hiram was often gruff, but he'd never before spoken to him in such an imperious manner.

Hiram dropped the book on his desk with an authoritative thwack.

"I need your help, Mister Mukherjee," Hiram said with more humility than Ravi had ever heard in his voice. "So decide this instant; do you want to go home or do you want to be part of something extraordinary?"

After the briefest moment's hesitation, almost before he realized he'd made a decision, Ravi found himself nodding his assent.

Hiram smiled. He clapped a heavy hand on Ravi's shoulder. "I knew you were a brave and noble lad. Excelsior, Mister Mukherjee. Truly." And then Hiram opened the notebook to a marked page toward the end, and therein explained to Ravi through his own words and sketches what it was he aimed to do.

"I've had an airship constructed from my own design. It's really quite spectacular in its own right, but it's only a tool built to carry the real object of our labors to an initial altitude of seventy-five thousand feet." He tapped two fingers on a sketch, presumably his own, depicting a dirigible unlike any Ravi had ever seen.

"The airship saves a surprising amount of fuel," Hiram was saying.

"At that height how do you—" Ravi started before Hiram cut him off with a snap of his fingers and firm rap on the page.

"Don't interrupt," said Hiram. He flipped to the next page, a simple sketch beside an indecipherable mass of figures on the opposite page.

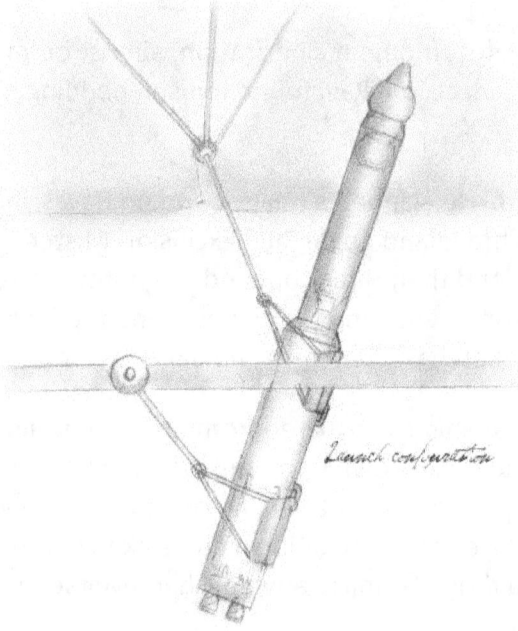

Launch configuration

"The occupants will be subjected to enormous acceleration. Nothing dangerous," Hiram assured Him. Ravi silently scoffed, as it sounded exceedingly dangerous.

"The first stage separates," Hiram said with a grumble. "And falls expensively back to Earth. Bloody inelegant but I suppose we must learn to stumble about before we can dance."

Ravi respectfully raised a hand for permission to speak but stopped in an instant at Hiram's angrily snapping fingers.

"The carriage is accelerated into an orbit by the second stage, which is then detached and left to orbit the Earth for as long as it will," Hiram said.

Ravi stared at the next illustration, depicting Mister Codon's spacecraft. It looked like a submersible built in the image of a peanut. Despite understanding at a glance the major details of the machine, Ravi questioned the sanity of anyone who would willingly attempt to pilot it.

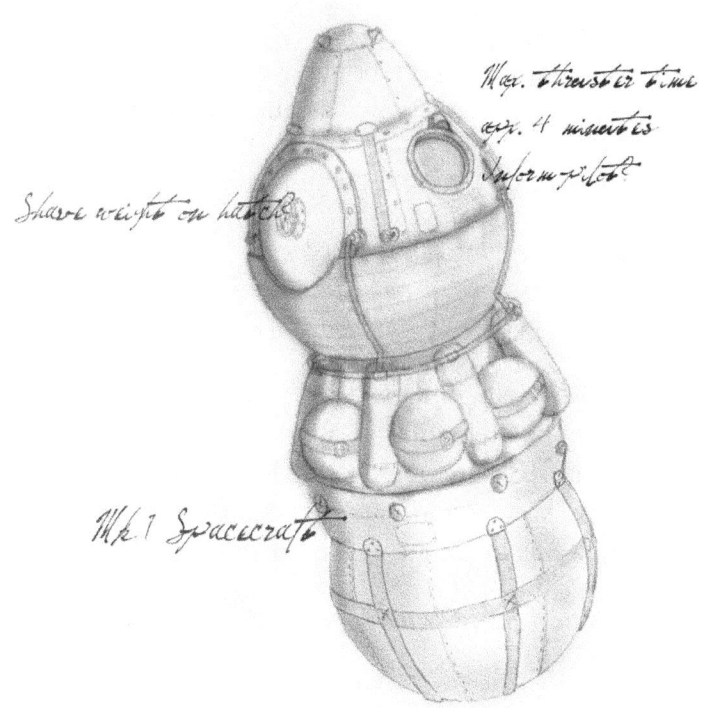

"At this point a number of scientific experiments are conducted, before the craft returns to Earth." Hiram turned the page to a sketch of the machine descending through clouds on three parachutes.

Ravi looked up from the page to Hiram, speechless.

"It is quite magnificent," Hiram said.

"It is quite mad," Ravi said.

"Everything innovative seems mad at first," said Hiram.

"For what do you need my help," Ravi asked. He felt a shudder creeping up on him.

"I've lost a pilot," Hiram said matter-of-factly. "I can't fly it alone."

"You. You and Major Westbridge were going to get in a box powered by what I can only assume was pure hydrogen peroxide?"

"And paraffin," Codon nodded.

"And be launched into space? Like a Jules Verne novel?"

Codon nodded again.

Somehow Ravi felt a bit less angry with Hiram over Javesh's death, knowing that he planned to risk the same death in his own unstable contraption. Hiram, however, at least knew the risks. The factory workers had known nothing other than that some unspecified danger was associated with the materials.

But Javesh had come to blow up the factory, Ravi thought. *He might have killed us all.*

Hiram may have been willing to pilot the thing, but Ravi wanted no part of hugging a giant jar of caustic liquid while being catapulted through the unknown realm of outer space.

"What about Doctor Wolfe?" asked Ravi, hating himself a little.

"Gunter?" Hiram asked, incredulous. "Well, he's not good with machinery."

"Or people," Ravi added.

Hiram's budding smile was suddenly snuffed out. Gazing out the office window, he opened his top desk drawer and produced a revolver.

"Nor trust, it would appear," he growled. "Come with me, Mister Mukherjee."

Ravi followed Hiram out to the airship, which was moored by a dozen heavy ropes outside its bulbous hangar. Without any conscious intent, Ravi had grabbed his suitcase on the way out, as he always did out of habit whenever he packed a bag and left it by the door.

Gunter was aboard the airship, frantically untying the mooring lines.

"Gunter, you swindling Teuton," Hiram shouted. "Get down from there!"

This only drove Gunter to work faster. The dirigible was beginning to tilt as the lines were unevenly released. "I should have done this a long time ago!" he shouted back as he tossed another rope aside.

Ravi turned at the sound of running feet behind him. Sophia was chasing, waving her arms frantically.

"They're coming?" she shouted.

"Who's coming," Ravi asked, trying to calm her.

"A mob!"

"Damn," Hiram winced. "I thought it would take them longer."

"What are you doing back here, Miss Westbridge?" Ravi asked, his frantic attention turned from Hiram's grandiose ambitions to Sophia's imminent danger.

"I came back to get my father's things but they. . . They're almost here!"

With his attention focused on Sophia, Ravi didn't notice that Hiram was rather ungracefully climbing up a mooring line to the unsteadily rising dirigible. Consequently, Ravi was startled when Sophia darted past him in mid-sentence.

"I'm giving you one chance to come to your limited senses," Hiram shouted, now clambering onto the deck, as he withdrew the revolver from his pocket. Ravi could not hear the last few words as they were drowned out by the sounds of breaking glass and breaking walls. The mob had arrived and was eagerly razing the factory.

"Did you really believe I was working for Britain," Gunter scoffed. "Working for you? Get off my ship!" Gunter drew a pistol of his own and fired two shots. Despite missing wildly, it was enough to send Hiram scampering for cover.

A shot rang out in response, again missing. "I see you're using Sam Colt's invention instead of your own," Hiram added.

The airship, which had been swaying around the last rope, pulled it up stake and all from the ground.

"For all your pretensions to genius you spend far too much time stealing the work of others," Hiram added, punctuating it with another errant shot from his revolver.

"Halt die klappe," Gunter shouted as he lunged at the controls, giving more power to the electric motors driving the props. He fired another shot in Hiram's general direction as the ship gained altitude.

Gunter was entirely unaware that Sophia had scrambled aboard, followed by Ravi, who was at that moment dangling precariously from the still-attached rope as the airship rose. From his elevated vantage point, Ravi could see the mob swarming over the factory with torches and hammers, destroying everything they could.

"Father," Sophia shouted. "We have to go back for him!"

"He is already on his way to the hospital," Ravi shouted back in an effort to calm her. "He is safe," Ravi added, as he dangled white-knuckled from the rope, now very high above the countryside. "I, however, am barely hanging on."

Sophia struggled to pull Ravi up when the factory exploded in a sun-like fireball. A surge of blistering hot air rose to buffet the entire airship, nearly sending Ravi and Sophia together over the deck. It was only by her mad grab that happened to connect with his shirt that she was able to stop his fall long enough for him to grab the rope and finish clambering aboard.

"Thank you, Miss Westbridge," Ravi said. She smiled. Warmth spread through him as if the sun had emerged from behind clouds.

"Pray don't mention it," she said, her cheeks dimpling. Her eyes drifted to the bag he was still somehow clutching, his knuckles white. "Always glad to help rescue a good set of luggage."

Ravi set the case down as Hiram fired his second to last shot several feet over Gunter's head.

While the two world-class engineers attempted to master the use of firearms, Sophia grabbed the control column and tried to steer the ship. The machine was remarkably fast for its size, once it got underway. It was also exceedingly sluggish about changing direction. Sophia overcorrected back and forth, resulting in a constant sway that both combatants found irritating.

Hiram had by then decided that he had very little to fear from Gunter's bullets, and made his way to Sophia, who had enlisted Ravi's help to fight the controls and further jerk the dirigible's deck about.

Whether out of some misleading intuition or simple panic, Sophia had pushed the steering column forward as though to make the ship move faster. This gesture instead angled the electric props to provide thrust forward and down at an angle of forty-fve degrees, which kept the airship at an excessively low altitude of several dozen feet. Over the countryside this was of little concern, but as they approached the outskirts of Kolkata it came to dominate their attention.

"Stand aside before you crash us into the Hooghly," Hiram shouted as he inserted himself between Sophia and the steering column.

"Nothing can lift both that rocket and your ego," Gunter shouted from behind cover.

"Doctor Wolfe—"

Gunter almost jumped. He hadn't seen Ravi approaching him from the other side.

"Please do stop that," Ravi added.

Gunter scowled and fired a shot at him. A hole appeared in the deck an arm's length from Ravi's left foot.

Ravi's eyes narrowed as he stomped authoritatively toward the German.

"I really cannot abide being shot at!"

Their confrontation was averted by the sound of Hiram's Webley revolver clicking on an empty cylinder.

"Bugger it all," he muttered.

Gunter let out a boisterous, mocking laugh. "A man who can't count to six trying to unravel the mysteries of Creation!"

Hiram threw the gun, at last connecting to Gunter's head with an authoritative thunk.

Out of reflex, Ravi attempted to catch the rebounding pistol before it fell overboard, but succeeding only in a passable impression of a clapping seal or cat batting at a string before the gun slipped from his grasp to fall on the streets not far below.

What Ravi did not know, though it might have pleased him greatly, was that at just that moment Maxwell Cullen had tromped outside to find out what everyone was standing around gawking at. His timing was such that the falling pistol, which had never once put a bullet on its intended target, now for the second time in as many minutes registered a solid hit with its frame.

"Fraud," Hiram shouted as he tackled Gunter. They wrestled on the deck with the same grace and skill exhibited in their attempt at a gunfight.

"English lapdog," Gunter retorted as he took the initiative in the grapple. Ravi and Sophia together pulled Gunter off Hiram and tried to restrain him. "Put me down you savage!"

Between his struggling, the wind, and the swaying deck, Sophia slipped and lost her grip. Gunter tumbled over the side to a largely harmless but gloriously humiliating landing in the Hooghly River.

"Bloody Visigoth," Hiram cursed as he brushed himself off. "Probably planning this all along."

Chapter

The sky was a patchwork of heavy grey storm clouds and indigo twilight. Once in a while a star would wink through, as if to reassure Ravi it was still there.

The further southwest they flew, the greyer the sky became. Still, they must be over or near an archipelago, because a large bird, some sort of heron or crane, kept pace with them for several minutes. Ravi watched the motion of its wings, both strong and delicate. The wind rippled over its feathers, the same zephyr that whipped through Ravi's hair. This had been Ravi's lifelong dream, to fly.

But now that he was in the air, he found himself pensive. Where was Hiram taking them? And what if the storm hit?

The bird does not worry about these things, thought Ravi. *The bird is caught up in the joy of flying.*

Sophia's clothes rustled as she came to stand next to him. She rubbed her arms, her teeth slightly chattering.

Ravi slipped off his coat and draped it around her shoulders.

"You are too much of a gentleman, Ravi. You'll freeze!"

"I am not bothered by cold, Miss Westbridge," he lied, unconvincingly.

"Since we've nearly escaped death together, I think you must call me Sophia," she said. She wrapped his coat tight around her shoulders.

She sighed heavily then, her breath fogging against the cold.

"What's wrong, Sophia?"

She seemed surprised he'd called her by her first name, despite that she had just now asked him to do so.

"It's father. Who will take care of him?"

"I'm sure he will have the finest doctors in all of India."

"But not his daughter to tend to him," she said. "All my life I wanted to be free of convention, to travel by dirigible, to have adventures. And now, I'm here, flying alongside the birds, and all I can think about it what a terrible daughter I am."

"That isn't so," said Ravi.

"Oh, but it is. If I hadn't been so curious, I wouldn't have provoked Gunter, and maybe none of this would have happened."

Ravi laughed. "Surely you don't mean to take responsibility for the actions of others? You might as soon take responsibility for the storm or the cholera. People know their own minds. The workers who started the fire do, and most certainly Gunter Wolfe does."

"I may not have started the fire, but I may have fuelled it," she said.

"Because you are curious? Without curiosity, there would be no airships. No ships of any sort. People would still be concerned with sailing over the edge."

"What are you curious about, Ravi?"

"Where Hiram is taking us," he said.

She smiled. "Me, too. What else?"

He looked out at the bird, who now broke off and spiraled downward toward whatever island had been its destination. "Heavier than air flight," he said.

She cocked her head, bird-like, waiting for him to continue. So he did. He told her about the Crystal Palace and Moy's aerial steamer, and how it had begun his obsession with flying machines. He told her about his proposal to use dirigibles to deliver cargo to the countryside. He told her about his own experiments and how each had failed, but how he had learned something each time.

"And now," said Ravi, "Hiram insists that he has designed a device capable not only of heavier than air flight, but of escaping the earth's atmosphere. It is... as fantastical as the vimanas in the legends of my people."

"Vimanas?" Sophia asked.

"Oh, yes, according to the old tales, the Gods and even some of the heroes used flying machines," he said.

"My father was supposed to pilot it, you know."

Ravi nodded.

"Do you think he will ask us to do it?"

"He cannot force us, Sophia."

"Force us? I will cajole him in every way I can think of to get into that machine."

Ravi regarded her for a few seconds and then burst into laughter.

"Are you amused?"

"I am certain that is not what a good daughter would do," said Ravi.

Sophia seemed momentarily offended, and then grinned broadly. "Perhaps not," she said. "I will make you a deal, Ravi. If you don't lose your curiosity, I won't lose mine. When Hiram asks you, and you know he will, are you going to agree to pilot the vimana?"

Before Ravi could answer, the deck began to shudder, followed by the sound of thumping feet. Hiram charged up like a wheezing rhino.

"I need you two lay-abouts back here," said Hiram.

"Why, is something wrong?" Sophia asked.

"Only that I've been at the helm for twenty-seven hours. Since I don't want to waste any match sticks by using them to prop my eyelids open, I'll need one of you to fly for a while."

"I can pilot the airship?" Sophia asked.

"Pilot, ha! I'll show you how to hold our course so we do not crash into the ocean," said Hiram.

Sophia eyeballed him. "Teach me to pilot the dirigible!" She demanded. "I plan to be the best pilot you have ever seen. What do you call this airship of yours, Mister Codon?"

"What's that? What do you mean, what do I call it?" Hiram huffed.

"Its name! I don't see it printed on the hull," she said.

Hiram shook his head. "I haven't time to come up with names for every tool and piece of machinery in the factory, Miss Westbridge. I doubt even Mukherjee would have the patience for such a task, or the memory. Go fetch Millicent, I'd say. Which one is Millicent? He'd ask. The mid-sized crank bolt wrench, I'd say. It would all just be confusing and entirely unhelpful."

"Charming," Sophia said, with a roll of her eyes. "I imagine you are a wonderful ballroom companion."

"We shall see, should I ever deign to set foot in a ballroom," Hiram replied.

"Where are we going, anyway?" demanded Ravi.

"Rhodesia by way of Mombasa," said Hiram.

"Rhodesia?" Ravi asked.

"Are you practicing to become a parrot, m'boy? Yes, Rhodesia! A charming place that a most uncharming man named after himself," said Hiram.

"We're going to Africa? How exciting, don't you think, Ravi?" Sophia bubbled.

Ravi shot her a dubious look.

"It should be clear sailing from here on," said Hiram. "Figuratively, of course."

With that, thunder rumbled through the storm clouds, and the last of the stars disappeared. A heavy raindrop hit Ravi's forehead with a wet slap.

"'Clear' being the figurative part?" he asked.

Shortly thereafter, the deluge began. In moments, the three occupants were drenched to the bone.

All signs of exhaustion gone, Hiram barked orders. "Take up the slack on the port side!"

Ravi raced to the pulley system, Sophia alongside of him.

"Sophia! Tighten that line!" yelled Hiram.

She hesitated, then grabbed the rope and pulled.

"I'll hold it taut, you knot it," Ravi shouted. She fumbled at first, but after a moment, tied a respectable knot.

She is not used to physical labor, thought Ravi. *Nor is she used to following orders.* And yet, here she was, working alongside him without complaint.

"There's land a few miles to starboard!" shouted Ravi. "Shouldn't we wait out the storm?"

"All the way or nothing!" Hiram returned, wiping rain from his goggles. "Tighten down the aft!"

Ravi darted toward the back of the ship.

The airship rocked with the driving rain and, at one point, hail. The storm pounded them for hours, with no signs of stopping. Ravi ran the length of the deck more times than he could count, and he felt every hour of his desk job in his screamingly sore arms and legs. Sophia, however, looked exhausted but also invigorated. Her wild curls whipped around her head like a gorgon, cracks of lighting illuminating her flushed cheeks. Her bicycle suit clung to her legs in an uncomfortable-looking but not unflattering way, and Ravi forced his eyes back to the rigging.

He drove himself to move faster, despite his protesting muscles. He would not seem weak in front of Sophia. *You care too much*, said an inner voice.

It was not until the first rays of morning sun backlit the grey horizon that the rainstorm wound down. Everything on the ship was drenched.

Deeply exhausted, Ravi was just about to sink to the deck for a much needed nap, when he noticed they were over land, and that there were people on it.

Relief flooded through him. When he lifted the spyglass, however, the relief was replaced by nausea and more than a little dread.

"Mister Codon," said Ravi to Hiram, who was flapping around his sodden bowler in a futile attempt to dry it off.

"Yes, yes, what is it?" Hiram said irritably.

"I do not believe those men are British."

Hiram turned from his hat to his equally sodden map. He slapped the compass down on top of it with a grunt. "Oh, bugger it all."

Ravi lifted the eyepiece and peered downward. A man who looked like a soldier peered back through his own spyglass. Ravi shifted the telescope to the soldier's insignia, which was, without a doubt, an Iron Cross.

His eyes drifted to the Union Jack on their stabilizing fins.

"Are we in German territory?" Ravi asked.

"No," said Hiram.

Ravi was about to protest, when Hiram said, "We're over German territory."

One of the soldiers raised a rifle.

"I don't mean to alarm you," he said, "but the Germans are pointing guns at us."

"I wouldn't worry about that," said Hiram. "We're much too high for them to shoot accurately, even if they were so inclined."

Three rifle shots rang out in the distance followed by a hiss from above. Ravi leaned back to look at one of the gas bladders, now leaking.

"Though we are very large," said Hiram.

The Germans unleashed another volley of shots, which resulted in another leak.

"Stop trying to reassure me. Every time you do the universe conspires to make things worse," shouted Ravi.

Sophia ran up, panting. "We're being shot at!" she yelled.

"We know!" Hiram and Ravi yelled in unison. Ravi glared at Hiram, who raised an eyebrow and glared right back.

"For a brilliant man you can be quite inept, Mister Codon," said Ravi.

"And for a civil servant you can be quite unhelpful," Hiram retorted. "Now tighten the cargo lines. I don't want the equipment damaged."

"What does it matter," spat Ravi, "the Germans will dismantle—"

"The Germans will not be a problem when we land," said Hiram.

"We're going to crash!" yelled Ravi.

"Yes. In British East Africa!" Hiram said triumphantly, enunciating each word.

"Forgive me if I do not take much comfort in your imaginary line as we plummet to our deaths!" shouted Ravi.

"You really need to relax, Mukherjee. And we need that machine."

Ravi and Sophia look toward the rocket, which gently swayed on its net of ropes and chains.

With resigned sighs Ravi and Sophia commenced securing the lines. Ravi glanced at the ground, still hundreds of feet below but getting closer.

"We are falling much too quickly," he said.

"At least we're not being shot at," she said.

Ravi grunted by way of affirmation.

"Ravi, look!" she said, grabbing the rigging and leaning dangerously over the side.

Ravi followed her eye line.

"Oh, no..." he said.

Below, a group of lions chased a herd of gazelles, trying to separate one out for the kill. Sophia's eyes shone.

"So close. It almost feels like I could touch them."

"I would not advise it," said Ravi.

Ravi flinched as Hiram let loose a mighty bellow. His legs were braced and his mouth frozen in a grimace as he pulled back on the gears. Hiram and the gears groaned in unison, as if they were part of the same organism, some flying mechanical pachyderm.

Ravi and Sophia lurched as the ship grazed the ground, and then lifted back up.

"Hold on to your hats!" Hiram shrieked.

Ravi tentatively put his arm around Sophia. "Don't worry, Sophia. Everything is going to be all right," he said. Hearing the tremor in his own voice, his heart sank at how not comforting his words were.

Sophia laughed out loud. "Please don't die, Ravi," she said. "You are far too magnificent."

The airship touched ground again, this time skidding across the ground throwing clumps of dirt, rock and sagebrush. Ravi pulled Sophia to him, guarding her head with one arm and his own with the other. He peered through his fingers. A tree was barreling at them at the speed of an angry bull elephant. Ravi braced himself as they hit, the impact reverberating through the deck, which fell away beneath them. Suddenly airborne, Ravi closed his eyes, Sophia's head still tucked to his chest. His shoulder thudded against the ground and he skidded several feet to an abrupt halt.

Ravi blinked, then patted himself down, surprised to be alive. He then turned to Sophia, who was wide-eyed, her shoulders shaking with hysterical laughter. He grinned, momentarily grateful even for the burning pain in his shoulder, which verified his aliveness.

Hiram grinned wide. "Ha!" he said, throwing his fist in the air. Then he said, "Mukherjee, come help me assess the damage done by the bloody Huns."

Hiram immediately scurried to the rocket, gingerly examining it. After only a moment, Hiram wheeled, eyes wider than Ravi had ever seen. He turned several shades of red, then white, then slightly green.

"Of all the—those bloody—" then words failed him and he let out a frustrated bellow.

"Are you quite all right Mister Codon?" Ravi asked.

"No, Mukherjee, I am not."

Hiram pulled out an aluminum ball, about the size of a human head. A bullet had pierced it, leaving it bent and inoperable.

"The gyroscope?" Ravi asked tentatively.

Hiram groaned by way of response.

Ravi remembered that this was a replacement part that had only been recently completed, and that it was the last piece of equipment required to launch. He also knew it had taken quite a long time to fabricate.

Hiram hurled the gyroscope at a nearby acacia tree, scattering a flock of birds.

Neither Ravi nor Sophia wanted to break the awkward silence.

Finally, Hiram's power of speech was restored. "Well, then," he said. "I'll just have to convince Cecil to build us an aluminum foundry and hire machinists so we can fashion another."

Ravi and Sophia exchanged doubtful glances. She winced.

"I hope you both have comfortable shoes, we have a walk ahead," said Hiram.

Ravi's shoulders sagged.

Chapter 9

If Ravi had the most comfortable shoes ever designed, he would still be trudging through sand. There was also very little shade on the coast, and he found himself wishing for more rain, despite the fact that his clothes were still slightly damp and were rubbing his skin in a most unpleasant fashion. He regretted that he did not have a simple kurta. He also wished, unreasonably so, that they would simply walk all the way to Rhodesia so he could stop plodding over sand and get under the shade of the acacia trees. Furthermore, he was not at all looking forward to meeting Rhodes.

The first part of the walk had not been bad. They had crashed a little further inland than they had supposed, but the African savannah was quite lovely. Still, it was eerily silent and Ravi could not shake the suspicion that there were eyes on them peeking out from behind trees and gentle hills.

Hiram, still beside himself over the gyroscope, had miscalculated the location of the town, which was now somehow south of their current location. Ravi had been the one to suggest returning to the coast and walking along it until they reached the coastal city of Mombasa.

Though when he caught the first glimpse of the town, relief flooded through him. *A bath!* he thought. Then dinner, and bed. Any bed that was not the deck of an airship. He was not picky. At least not right then.

The English-style buildings of Mombasa punctuated mangroves and tall tropical trees. Ravi first noticed a frontier-like quality. Englishmen, Arabs, Indians and Africans went about their business. Perhaps he wouldn't seem as peculiar as he'd feared.

Hiram looked Sophia over, as if she were a malfunctioning piece of machinery.

"Oh, this will not do," he said, shaking his head. "This will not do at all."

"What will not do?" she demanded, indignant.

"Your attire, my dear."

"Excuse me, Mister Codon! Aside from the fact that you are hardly as fresh as a daisy yourself, it is really quite ungentlemanly of you to mention it!"

"You mistake my meaning, my dear, but you are quite right. We are all in need of a bit of freshening. Come!"

****

Ravi glanced from Hiram, who was waiting just outside the doorway with uncharacteristic patience, and Cecil Rhodes, who had yet to acknowledge their presence as he held his quill over a page, pondering the precise wording a letter's conclusion. He sat behind a solid, finely crafted but rather plain desk that was cluttered with correspondence. Behind him a window looked out over Mombasa, seemingly containing the entire settlement within its border.

"Come in, Hiram," Cecil said, still writing. "Sit." He signed the letter, folded it, then at last the round face of Cecil Rhodes looked up at them. He waited silently with eyes fixed on Hiram, not acknowledging Ravi or Sophia at all.

"Mister Rhodes. This is Ravi Mukherjee, my manservant."

Ravi bristled. Fortunately for the ruse, Cecil seemed utterly unconcerned with him.

"And this young man," Hiram continued, sweeping an open hand toward Sophia wearng Rav's suit and Hiram's soggy bowler, "is Robert Westbridge."

Sophia nodded and smiled in what she thought was a manly fashion. She was badly mistaken.

"Not quite how I'd pictured you, Major," Cecil said, looking her over. "Pleased to meet you at last. I trust you are up to the task?"

"The food in India doesn't agree with the Major," Hiram offered. "He's been ill, but the good Major has recovered and is ready to make history, isn't that right old Bob?"

"For King and Country," Sophia bellowed in a forced baritone. Ravi stifled a laugh.

"I hear that in India you've had disagreements with more than the food," Cecil said in a dry, serious tone.

"We all have challenges we must overcome," Hiram replied. "India has come a long way toward civilization in the past few years." Only Sophia noticed Ravi's glance.

"Your machine is here?"

"A few miles south, in actuality," Hiram said. His hands clasped together, fingers fluttering off nervous energy. "Some overzealous Germans caused a great deal of damage."

"I see," Cecil said with all the judgment of a disappointed father. "What do you need?"

As if he'd been waiting for the cue, Hiram pulled a list from his pocket. He unrolled it with a crisp snap, pinched the ends for rigidity, and handed it across the desk.

Cecil Rhodes read the list slowly, his eyes scanning back and forth, his face utterly expressionless. Finally he set it on the desk, but said nothing for a moment.

"Why should I build you a foundry?"

"They irreparably damaged our guidance gyroscope," Hiram said. Cecil seemed entirely unmoved. "It's a very precise piece of aluminum machinery. Gunter's Germans provided the original, but obviously they'll be no help."

"I seem to recall having paid for a replacement once before."

Ravi had never seen Hiram flustered before. He hid it well, but Ravi had spent enough time with him to see it.

"I wonder if it might be cheaper to simply annex German Africa than build you new factories every time you break something," Cecil said in a dry tone that made it impossible to tell if he was scolding or joking.

Hiram seemed about to answer, but refrained.

Cecil settled back into his chair. He glared at Hiram for a long moment during which Ravi could sense the calculations going on in both their heads.

These two white men, Ravi thought, silently seething. *Plotting the future for the rest of the world, whether anyone else wants it or not.*

"I am a student of history," Cecil said at last. "Territory and resources. Our great object is to control as much of both as possible. Now, to think of these stars that we see overhead at night and know that they are worlds without count." He looked at Hiram. His cleft chin tightened into his round face as though bracing for something. "And that you might bring us to the very cusp of reaching them. Might."

Ravi glanced between the two men, both brilliant in their own ways. Both supremely arrogant.

"It makes me sad to see them so clear and yet so far. I would annex the planets for Britain if I could."

"Of that I have no doubt," Hiram answered. Ravi was sure he detected the slightest hint of mockery in Hiram's voice. "It seems a wise investment," Hiram added.

"If you can do it," Cecil answered. He dropped his hands onto his desktop with a clap of finality. "I'll not be giving you another farthing until you can demonstrate this contraption of yours is anything more than another fantastical flying machine that only works inside a madman's head."

"Mister Rhodes," Hiram protested. "Allow me to repair what we've already built, at least. We can't throw away years of work!"

"I won't throw away a fortune on a fool's errand. Can you offer me something more than grand proclamations?"

"I... This project..." Hiram gasped, and then went silent as he carefully considered what response had the greatest chance of securing further funding, regardless of what was, strictly speaking, true.

"The Germans," Ravi offered. All eyes turned to him.

"Yes," Hiram bellowed, seizing on the lifeline. "Germans! That devious Hun Gunter Wolfe has been pilfering my research for years. Are you willing to let the Huns beat Britain to the planets?"

"Your airship," Rhodes said after some consideration. "Can it be repaired and flown to Salisbury?"

"Most assuredly."

"One carriage of supplies, then," Cecil offered. "I think that's generous under the circumstances."

"Barely adequate," Hiram answered. "But we must make do."

****

Hiram insisted upon going into the pub to wait for the supply carriage. *Apparently*, Ravi thought, *being told no is enough to drive him to drink*.

The ambient noise level fell to a murmur when the three walked through the door. The patrons were exclusively white and male, most of them in military uniforms and pith helmets. The sidelong glances Ravi received from under those helmets were not lost on him.

"My good fellows!" bellowed Hiram. Ravi was amused to find that Hiram did not fit in here any better than himself and Sophia. She crouched down under her hat and coughed.

A few grunted before going back to their drinks.

Ravi and Sophia took an unobtrusive seat by a window while Hiram trundled over to the bar.

"My goodness, what a difficult man," Sophia said under her breath.

"Codon is the most difficult man I have ever met," Ravi said. "And that includes my last supervisor, which is saying something."

Sophia laughed. "Yes, I suppose he is, but I was speaking of Rhodes. He makes my father seem positively jolly. All that about annexing the planets. I say! We don't even know what's there."

Ravi was about to respond when Hiram returned with three pints.

"Here you are, my good men," he said, with a wink at Sophia.

Ravi shook his head. Sophia took a tentative sip, then grimaced. "Do you men really enjoy drinking this stuff?" she said in a loud whisper.

"You'll notice that most of us men in this pub do," Hiram said pointedly, as if reminding her that she was still wearing Ravi's trousers.

"Not all of us men do," Ravi said, glowering. "Thank you for asking."

"Come now, my friend, why so glum?" Hiram said, with a slap on the shoulder.

"Your friend?" Ravi said incredulously. "An hour ago you introduced me as your manservant."

"That was what Rhodes expected. It's easier to get things from people if you tell them what they want to hear," said Hiram.

Ravi was not pacified. "I directed a department for three years at ICS. I am no one's manservant," he grumbled. He was ready to continue, to tell Hiram exactly what he thought of him and of Rhodes when Sophia gasped.

"Look!" she said.

Ravi leaned forward to peer out the window. A lion was sitting in the middle of the street, looking straight at them.

Ravi was so startled he stood. Sophia, mistaking his alarm for excitement, stood as well, putting her hand on his elbow. This was as startling to Ravi as the lion, but he did not move away.

"It's beautiful," she said.

"And it's in the middle of town," he said.

Several of the pith-helmeted patrons craned their necks to see what the fuss was about.

"A lion!" one of them shouted. "Hand me my rifle, quickly!"

The soldier and two of his compatriots ran outside.

"Wait!" shouted Sophia, but they did not listen. She dashed after them, followed closely by Ravi and Hiram.

They rounded the corner just in time to see the soldier lift his rifle and fire. The crack echoed through the streets. The lion's roar turned into a pathetic whimper, full of pain. Another soldier fired. The iron smell of blood filled the air as the lion collapsed to the ground. Sophia's eyes glistened.

"Why kill it?" she asked Ravi.

More of the pub patrons filed out, cheering for the soldier and congratulating him on the kill.

"But it just stood there," she complained. "It didn't attack."

"The fur is valuable," said Hiram. "And they were afraid of the beast."

"It had more right to be here than they do," said Ravi. "It's a native of this land."

A few of the soldiers carried off the lion carcass. Disgusted, Ravi turned to walk away. Sophia and Hiram followed.

"Ravi, where are you going?" she asked.

"Back to India," said Ravi.

"On foot?" Hiram demanded.

Ravi wheeled. "You might think I am a stupid manservant, but I know how to buy passage on a ship."

"There's no reason for this, my good man," said Hiram.

"There is every reason for it." Ravi began walking again, then stopped suddenly, remembering that he'd planned to give Hiram an earful earlier.

"Have you given any thought to how your inventions will be used, Mister Codon?"

"Please don't tell me you are indulging superstitions about the evils of science," scoffed Hiram.

Ravi, tempted to use very ungentlemanly language, took a deep breath before continuing. "I'm the one you brought on the project, ostensibly because of my..." he affected Hiram's voice and manner as he said, 'penchant for scientific knowledge, outside the envelope.'"

"And now you're having second thoughts," said Hiram.

"You should be having second thoughts!" said Ravi.

"I told you this is going to work."

"And what if it does? What if Rhodes actually annexes the planets?"

"Nonsense."

"Or what if he has you build a lightning gun airship?"

"Ridiculous!"

"No. It isn't. If I realize that you have the capacity to build it, then it's only a matter of time before Rhodes does as well. And if you think that Gunter hasn't already thought of it, then you are more of an idealist than I thought," said Ravi. Then he paused, the obvious finally occurring to him. "Oh no, that's it, isn't it?"

"What's it?"

"For all your brilliance and quick wit, you are a dreamer with your head in the clouds. You have no idea of the implications of your work," he said. He sighed deeply before continuing. "I will tell you something I have known since I was a boy. Science is an extremely powerful tool that can be used for the benefit of humanity, or to its detriment."

Hiram remained silent, waiting for him to continue.

"You don't really believe that Rhodes is going to allow you to keep your inventions to yourself upon their completion, do you?"

"I have no intention of..."

"Hasn't it occurred to you that when Gunter finally presents the Kaiser with his Iron Wolfe and whatever other instruments of death he's devising, that the British government will demand the same? Making your Scramble of Africa even worse? Look around! You Europeans running amok shooting at each other, making power plays for land that's already occupied!"

Ravi, having no idea if his words were having an impact, resumed walking. He shouted the last over his shoulder. "I will not be a party to it. To using science as a tool of oppression. On this world or on any other."

"Ravi, wait!" Sophia said, running up to him.

He stopped.

"There's potential for great things to come of this, too," she said. "Think of it! If we could communicate with America from here. A rapid exchange of information could facilitate so much good! Not to mention exploring the stars, and finding out what the aether is really made of!"

"And whether it exists at all," Hiram cut in.

"I don't trust Rhodes," said Ravi.

"Ha! I don't either," said Hiram. "But we can still do good things with his money."

"Assuming he elects to give you any!" Ravi said.

"Ravi, wait," Sophia said. "Don't you want to see if the vimanas can be real? Don't you want to fly through the heavens?"

Fly through the heavens like Sri Rama. It was a child's fantasy. And yet...

"Sophia, that contraption is very dangerous. You should not go up in it. No one should," he said, though he heard his own lack of conviction in his voice.

"If we don't, then Gunter will," said Sophia. "You said it, yourself. Remember what you said about curiosity, Ravi. You promised if I didn't give up, you wouldn't, either."

Ravi looked at Sophia's pleading eyes, too large for her freckled face.

Still torn, a horse-drawn carriage pulled up, piled with canvas, crates and pressurized tanks.

"Our benefactor comes through at last. Well, m'boy, it's time to make your choice. Are you coming?"

He did not want to make this choice because of a woman and her lovely green eyes. He'd seen many men ruined for such choices. But what she'd said about Gunter struck a chord. That vile man, the first person in space? Wasn't that the reason he himself had given Rhodes for why Hiram's project should continue to be funded?

He met Sophia's gaze, nodded once, and headed toward the carriage.

Chapter 10

Ravi loosened his tie and patted his face with a kerchief. He didn't care for Sophia to see him perspiring in his grey suit.

He needn't have been concerned, however, as Sophia was flushed and fanning herself quite vigorously. A honey blonde curl stuck to her neck, sweat pooling around it. She fidgeted, trying to obtain the maximum air flow through her attire, which was still largely Ravi's. Hiram was sweating profusely and unabashedly waving his bowler around in an attempt to cool off.

"Damnable sun is trying to kill me," he complained.

"Perhaps if you Europeans hadn't invented such uncomfortable clothing... " said Ravi, who didn't find British clothing particularly uncomfortable, but knew that most people did, including the British.

"If I had invented it, I guarantee you it would be far more efficient," grumbled Hiram.

"All those seamstresses and all that silk, and you couldn't manage to engineer one decent pair of trousers or a smart dress," said Sophia.

"And who would wear such a dress, might I ask?" said Hiram, with a wink.

Ravi heard a rustling from a nearby copse of trees. He thought he caught something out of the corner of his eye, but when he turned his head, he saw nothing. He remembered his sense of being watched when they had been on their way into the city.

"What is it?" Sophia asked.

Ravi shook his head. "I'm not sure. Possibly nothing."

They continued, Ravi peering from side to side. As they passed the next group of trees, Ravi saw eyes. Human eyes.

He leaned to Hiram. "I believe we are being watched," he said.

"We'd best keep moving," Hiram replied. "We'll be there within the hour."

Ravi flipped open his watch.

True to Hiram's word, they were at the site of the crashed airship in exactly fifty-nine minutes. However, the rocket carriage was empty.

Ravi noticed tracks made by wheels from a caravan. His eyes followed the wheel rut, which was very clearly headed south.

Hiram, who saw the same tracks, lifted binoculars and continued to follow the tracks as they led into German East Africa.

"Well, I'll be stuffed and wrapped in bacon," he said.

The Maasai warrior Legishon peered through the space between two boulders. The three of them, the two pink-faces and the other one, had reached the debris. He and his small band of warriors had been tracking them all afternoon. Yesterday, they had seen the others come and go. Also, pink faces. Sankei told him they were not British, that he could tell by the different decorations on their clothes, like Maasai knew the other tribes by their beadwork. But Legishon could not tell. The pink faces all looked British to him.

"What is that one?" Kapalei asked.

"Another wazungu," muttered Sankei.

"No, he's different. From a northern tribe?" Kapalei suggested.

Legishon shook his head. "I do not think so. He is not like us. But he is not like the British, either."

"What does it matter? He is with them," Sankei insisted.

Kapalei shrugged. "What about her? She is no warrior, she is just a woman."

"They are fewer than the others, and less well-armed. I say we kill them now, while we have the advantage of surprise," said Sankei.

Legishon shook his head, again. Sankei was hotheaded, which is why the tribe never chose him to lead the warriors. But he had reason to dislike the British. Legishon could see the angry scar near Sankei's shoulder and the other in his leg. Sankei still moved with a very slight limp, but he was quick and almost graceful. Legishon was glad to have him as an ally, hotheaded or no.

"I do not think we need to kill them. We can take them back to the elders."

"What about the noisy one?" Kapalei said.

"We can kill him and take the others prisoner," said Sankei.

Kapalei nodded.

"Let us see what he does. If he comes peaceably, let us not kill him, but if he resists," said Legishon. He did not need to finish the thought.

****

The sun hung low in the sky, spreading red and gold across the horizon. The savannah erupted in the lively sounds only heard at sunset. Sophia was fast asleep on deck, using a burlap sack of cornmeal as a pillow. Ravi assisted Hiram in taking inventory of the stores and evaluating damage to the ship.

"Be a good lad and hold that lantern for me," said Hiram.

Ravi shot Hiram an annoyed look, which Hiram did not see because he was bent over, rummaging through a supply cabinet.

Ravi bit back a comment about this being Hiram's good side, and merely said, "I would be grateful if you would stop referring to me as lad."

"No offence meant, good sir. I am a number of years older than you. Sooner or later, you'll find yourself doing it as well."

The lantern shone brightly in the increasing darkness, and Ravi looked uncomfortably about. It was like a beacon attracting bugs, at the very least, and quite likely something larger. Also, he had never shaken the feeling that they were being followed. It wasn't so much the occasional crack of twigs or what sounded like rustling of clothing, but the feeling that eyes were on him. He hoped he was just being paranoid, that it was the unfamiliarity of the environment, but the sinking feeling in his stomach was not reassuring.

"I hope you are almost finished," he said.

"Good news," said Hiram, poking his head out. "The good doctor left everything but the rocket. The damage isn't quite as extensive as I had feared, and it seems, by some miracle, the ship hasn't been raided by anyone else."

Ravi peered around, eyes honing in on a pair of boulders leaning against each other.

"What is it, Mukherjee? You look as though you'd seen a ghost."

"There's something over there," Ravi whispered.

"Nonsense, it's the night sounds playing tricks on you," said Hiram. He jumped down and sauntered around the boulders. Momentarily, he emerged from the other side, accompanied by five Maasai warriors aiming spears at him. Hiram had his hands in the air.

"Or perhaps it was these fellows," he said sheepishly.

Ravi nudged Sophia awake with his toe. She leapt to her feet with a strangled sound as fifteen more Maasai emerged, seemingly out of nowhere. *Apparently, their reputation for stealth is well-deserved*, Ravi thought, raising his arms.

"My good fellows," Hiram began. An angry looking young man lifted a spear to Hiram's throat. Ravi could see he had several scars.

"No need for that," Hiram continued, "if you will just allow me to..." He tried to lower his arm to reach into his pocket, but the man shouted something in his native tongue.

Another of the men gestured for the first to back off. The scarred young man grabbed Hiram by the arm.

"My word!" muttered Hiram, wrenching free. The rest of the Maasai advanced on Hiram, spears drawn.

Ravi leapt in front of Hiram, arms outstretched. "Please don't kill him!" He cried. A half second later, when Ravi himself was facing twenty spearheads, he wondered what had possessed him.

"Why not?" said one of the Maasai, who appeared to be the leader.

"You speak English," said Ravi.

The Maasai warrior grunted, nodding. "Why should I not kill him?"

"Because I can't have the madman's death on my conscience!"

The Maasai looked at Hiram doubtfully. "You say he is mad?"

"Yes, truly an escapee from Bedlam!"

"I say!" Hiram said.

"If you're smart, you'll say nothing at all," Ravi muttered under his breath.

"He doesn't seem like a madman," said the Maasai.

"Why else do you think he talks so much? He talks and he talks, but he makes no sense, I assure you."

Hiram harrumphed.

"And you?" said the Maasai. "What are you?"

"I?" Ravi asked.

"Yes. What is your tribe?"

Ravi blinked.

"Tell them where you are from, Mukherjee," Hiram whispered.

"Oh, I am from India," said Ravi. "Who are you?"

The Maasai seemed taken aback as he said, "I am the warrior Legishon."

Legishon turned and spoke to his fellows. They laughed. He looked back at Ravi. "So we have a woman, a madman, and you."

The Maasai broke into a heated discussion in their own language. The one with the scars spoke the loudest, banging his spear on the ground.

"Might I ask what they are saying?" Ravi asked.

"We have been discussing whether or not to kill you," said Legishon.

Hiram and Sophia made eye contact, alarmed.

"Might I ask what you are deciding?" asked Ravi.

"Fortunately for you, we are not in the habit of killing women, madmen, or men from India."

Ravi visibly relaxed.

"But we will have to figure out what to do with you while we investigate your flying machine."

"Wha—OW!" Hiram shouted, the word turning into a howl of pain as Ravi kicked him in the leg.

The Maasai looked on dubiously.

"Madman," Ravi said. "Pity him."

"Please walk this way," said Legishon. The other Maasai surrounded them, urging them forward with their spears. Ravi saw movement out of the corner of his eye. When he turned to look, he saw the young, scarred warrior, slipping away.

****

Gunter gritted his teeth as a group of soldiers, using cranes made from logs and simple pulleys, vertically positioned his rocket on top of a twenty-five foot high wooden platform. The enormous structure had a set of wooden stairs up both sides and a ladder reaching to the capsule. Every time the soldiers adjusted something, every time the rocket moved even a fraction of an inch, Gunter cringed.

It had been his idea to launch from the edifice. This was the best way, he knew, not from the ground, or worse yet, mid-airship flight like that idiot Codon insisted. The rocket required ideal and controllable conditions, which the airship could not provide. Still, although Gunter knew that the platform was stable, it did not entirely look it, and he experienced a twinge of doubt.

Gunter also wished he had direct supervision of the soldiers, who rolled their eyes at him each time he told them to do something. It was true that he was not in the military, but the project was funded by the Kaiser, himself, and that should count for something.

The soldiers reported to Hauptman Oskar von Rauch, who looked every inch the aristocratic military officer. Rauch leaned lazily against the side of a building and smoked a cigarette as he watched. Gunter did not appreciate Rauch's cavalier attitude.

One of the soldiers let go a chain, which clanged off the rocket. Gunter winced.

"You!" he shouted. "Be careful! That represents many years of work!"

The soldier threw Gunter a dirty look and glanced balefully at Rauch.

"I would think," said Rauch, "Years of work would be deserving of something more than a wood pile for support."

Gunter bit his tongue. Weren't there any military scientists available? Rauch was both insufferable and an idiot. "Ground clearance," he said. "We need it up to launch."

"How soon?" asked Rauch.

"Three days, Hauptmann Rausch, at the very most," Gunter responded.

Rauch looked thoughtful for a moment, taking a long drag on his cigarette before crushing it out with his heel. "If any of my contingent die on this contraption," he said slowly, looking Gunter in the eye, "this will be your funeral pyre."

Gunter laughed uneasily. He had no doubt that Rauch meant it.

"The Kaiser himself has approved my plans," he said, his usual haughtiness sounding hollow, even to himself. "You should have a little more faith."

"I have as much faith in your scheme as the Kaiser does," Rauch said wryly.

Gunter glanced up to see the rocket angled backward. He grunted.

"A little more forward! There, stop!" Gunter yelled. He turned to Rauch. "Now, Hauptmann, if you will collect my gyroscope."

Rauch looked at him blankly.

Gunter felt his face flush, his stomach sinking.

"The aluminum ball," he elaborated, gesturing to show the size.

Oskar smirked, raising an eyebrow.

"Surely you found it! That schwachkopf dropped it right under your noses!" Gunter yelled, forgetting himself.

"This is not a nursery, Herr Doktor," said Rauch. "I suggest you learn to keep track of your own things."

Rauch turned his heel and stalked away.

Chapter

Ravi's primary thought as he sat tied to a pole with his back to Hiram and Sophia was, *I hope I am not sitting in cow dung.*

The absurdity of it was not lost on him. A sane person would be bemoaning his imminent death or trying to figure a way out of it. But no, Ravi Mukherjee was worried about his trousers.

The small village consisted of several star-shaped or circular mud huts, and a fairly large group of cows inhabiting an enclosure near the village center. This was both literal as well as metaphorical, as the Maasai lifestyle revolved around the herding of cattle.

As far as prisons went, the security was not much. The village was surrounded by a fence made from acacia, which Ravi assumed was meant to keep cattle in, not people. A bored and yawning guard stood several feet away, spending as much time watching a group of young women chatting and laughing as they strung beads than watching the three prisoners.

"See if you can twist your hand," said Hiram. "Ow! Not that way, the other way."

"Oh, it's no use," said Sophia. "Even if we do manage to wriggle out of here, everyone in the village is staring at us."

"They have to sleep, sometime," said Hiram.

"But they keep guards," said Sophia.

The guard had meandered over to the women and seemed to be trying to flirt, with only moderate success.

"Oh, I think we can handle him," said Hiram.

"It would be a mistake to underestimate the Maasai, Mister Codon," said Sophia.

"He is talking again. Anything that begins with him talking is likely to be a mistake," mumbled Ravi.

"Me? You're the one that's always disagreeable. Didn't anyone ever tell you that complaining is unproductive? Now everybody turn your hands counter-clockwise on the count of three."

Annoyed, Ravi deliberately yanked his hand clockwise.

Hiram cried out, and a few of the Maasai women looked up from their beadwork.

"Poor tortured soul," said Ravi.

"There has got to be something in this village that can help us," Sophia said.

"Doubtful," said Hiram. "They live in huts made of mud and cow dung."

"I was perfectly happy not knowing that," Ravi said, thinking again of his trousers.

"Go ahead and peer around, if you'd like," said Hiram. "It's not like these huts are doubling as roundhouses for locomotives."

Ravi peered around, anyway. What Hiram said was true. The Maasai's level of technology was low. But Sophia was correct, also. Surely between the three of them they could come up with something.

"Perhaps we can make a daring escape by galloping out on a few of the cattle." said Hiram.

A small child emerged from a hut across from him. He was carrying a sphere, roughly nine inches in diameter, which glinted in the sun. Ravi's eyes narrowed. "Mister Codon, where was it that you lost the original gyroscope?"

"What's that?" Hiram muttered.

"I wish I'd seen Mister Houdini a few more times to figure out how he works these knots," Sophia said, flustered.

"I am not Houdini, but I still think..." Hiram began again.

"Hush. Look at that boy," said Ravi.

Hiram scoffed. "Oh, for the love of—Mukherjee, the Germans have the original gyroscope. It fell right into their hands last time I was in Africa."

"Then the Maasai have much greater technological abilities than we suspect," Ravi said wryly, "because the object that child is carrying looks remarkably similar to the one you threw at the birds."

Hiram craned his neck painfully in order to see. His jaw dropped.

"Well, I'll be a red-bottomed baboon," said Hiram.

"Something else I did not need to know," Ravi said, with a roll of his eyes.

"I need that gyroscope!" said Hiram.

Sophia twisted around. "Where in the world did that child come by it?"

"As good a question as that is, Sophia dear, it is immaterial. What is, in fact, material, is that he has it and I need it," said Hiram.

Ravi did not speak the language of the Maasai, but he only had one idea. He shouted to the Maasai women.

"Excuse me, ladies?" he said.

The group of women looked over, suspiciously. One of them, an unusually tall woman, got up and approached them. Like the others, she wore bright colors and a lot of beaded jewelry.

"Can you understand me?" he asked.

She looked at him vaguely, not comprehending.

"Water? Thirsty?" Ravi tried to think of a way to mime drinking water while his hands were tied and realized that this was a worse idea than he'd originally thought.

His eyes drifted to a bucket of water. He could see a glimmer of understanding in her eyes. She headed over to the bucket.

"I hope this works, Mukherjee. If she unties us, we'll grab the gyroscope and make a run for it," said Hiram.

Ravi was just letting himself get his hopes up when they heard the Maasai warriors returning. They talked and laughed loudly, and Ravi saw that they carried most of the removable contents of the airship.

Hiram groaned.

Legishon held Gunter's Iron Wolfe. First he lifted it vertically, then horizontally. He held it like a baton, a quarterstaff, and then brought it to his shoulder as if it were an actual rifle. After several minutes, he held it like Gunter had, peering through the brass scope. He aimed at a nearby rock and pulled the trigger. Ravi expected to hear the crack and sizzle of the charge, but nothing happened.

"This is a weapon, madman, is it not?" Legishon demanded.

Hiram said nothing.

"Answer!"

"Yes, of sorts," said Hiram.

"More British weapons brought here to kill us?" said Legishon angrily.

"No, that is the only one of its kind, and I assure you it was not brought here to kill you," said Hiram.

Legishon lifted it up as if to bludgeon Hiram with it.

"He's telling the truth!" Ravi burst out. "It is a prototype."

Legishon inspected it further. "How do you make it work?" he said.

"If I show you, what do I get in return?" asked Hiram.

Legishon looked incredulous. "Your life, madman! Isn't that enough?"

"Almost, but not quite," said Hiram. "Don't worry," he quickly added. "I want nothing unreasonable. You see that ball that boy is holding?" Hiram said.

Legishon and the other warriors turned. Ravi noticed the young, scarred man had rejoined the warriors. When he saw the young boy holding the ball, he hurried over, yelling at him. The boy appeared confused at first, then handed the man the ball, sheepishly, looking like he would like to cry, but would not.

The young man stormed over to Legishon, yelling all the while.

"My friend Sankei says the price is too high. He says he hoped to get a hundred rifles for such an object, which is undoubtedly very rare and valuable to you," said Legishon.

"No offense, but he is not aware of the comparative value of the objects. I tell you, you are the ones coming out ahead in this deal," said Hiram.

Ravi tried not to roll his eyes.

Legishon turned to Sankei. The two of them argued.

"Ahem," said Hiram. "Since you have already taken everything else I own," he nodded to the loot from the airship, "I can hardly offer you more. However, under the circumstances, our lives, all three of them, and that small ball, are hardly too much to ask in return for the knowledge of how to use that weapon."

Legishon and Sankei argued some more. Finally, Legishon turned to them. "Done," he said. Sankei, livid, turned heel and stomped off.

True to his word, Hiram showed Legishon how to use the Iron Wolfe. Hiram aimed the weapon at an acacia tree and pulled the trigger. A crack and sizzle filled the air as lightning shot out from the barrel, cracking the tree in half.

"You can also reduce the setting," said Hiram.

Before Hiram could show him how, Legishon aimed and fired. Another tree cracked in half. The rest of the Maasai cheered.

No one should have that much power, Ravi thought. *Not Rhodes, not Gunter, and not these people.*

"Well, nice doing business with you," said Hiram. "If you're satisfied we've met our end of the bargain, we'll be leaving, now."

Legishon turned and sized Hiram up. Then he said, "You are free to go."

Hiram hustled Ravi and Sophia out of the village. When they were out of eyesight, Hiram grabbed Ravi's arm with his left hand and Sophia's arm with his right and broke into a run.

"We'd better hurry up before the thing stops working," he said.

"How long is that going to be?" asked Sophia.

"Any time now," said Hiram.

"I can't believe you showed them how to use that!" Ravi yelled.

"What does it matter? It's a pile of junk, and it only has four charges left. I'll warrant that they'll use all of them decimating trees," said Hiram. "We just don't want to be around when they figure it out."

Ravi picked up his pace.

By the time the three made it to the airship, they were all winded. Ravi made a cursory attempt to compose himself, then decided it was wasted effort. Sophia, on the other hand, had untucked her shirt and rolled up her pant legs in a way that was unbefitting of either a lady or a gentleman, and was trying to fan herself with her helmet.

"After spending so much time in men's clothing, I may never go back," said Sophia.

Hiram harrumphed. Ravi did not add that men's clothing somehow flattered her, drawing attention to her feminine curves in a rather immodest manner. He did not understand how Rhodes or anyone else could have been fooled by the disguise.

"How is it that Mukherjee here seems to avoid perspiration?" grumbled Hiram, as he took stock of what was missing from the airship. "Gah! They're like magpies! Everything with the slightest bit of sheen has gone missing."

"But can we fix it?" asked Ravi.

"Yes. I believe so. With some improvisation and a great deal of work. And very little time, of course," said Hiram, peering over his shoulder. He clapped his hands. "Roll up your sleeves, my friends! No rest for the weary."

12
Chapter

Gunter and Oskar approached the Maasai village on horseback, accompanied by a small contingent of soldiers.

"You're sure it's here?" Gunter said doubtfully.

"No, I'm not sure," Oskar said, "but my source is reliable, and he seems to think it is."

"It will have to be completely stripped and recalibrated," Gunter said doubtfully. "It's a precision instrument, not a bludgeon."

Oskar slowed, looking hard at Gunter. "Then we will salvage what we can. I see no reason to squander resources to build a complex piece of equipment if there is one at our disposal."

Gunter scoffed. "A Maasai village in British territory is hardly at our disposal. Assuming your source is correct."

Oskar did not respond, but merely spurred his horse to a gallop, leaving Gunter behind with the other soldiers.

Gunter moved to keep up. In the distance, a lone Maasai warrior approached. After a few moments, he saw a group of them following a short distance behind.

Oskar slowed, as did the rest of the contingent. The lone warrior was angrily spouting something in his native tongue, which, oddly, Oskar seemed to understand.

"I see," he murmured.

As the group of Maasai approached, Gunter saw that one of them held the Iron Wolfe. *His* Iron Wolfe. Gunter spurred his horse forward.

"What are you doing with my state of the art piece of machinery, you miserable savages? Hand it over at once!" he spat.

The leader fired. As he did so, a deafening crack filled the air, and an acacia tree next to Gunter split in half and fell over. Gunter's horse reared back and threw him, galloping off in a panic. Gunter swiveled his head this way and that, looking for cover, but the other soldiers were trying to steady their horses which were all prancing about in fear. There were no rocks or trees within an easy leap.

"Don't shoot!" he cried, instantly ashamed of his weakness.

The warrior who had first approached had tumbled to the left and was now watching from safely behind a boulder.

The leader continued advancing on Gunter, looking far more formidable than Gunter ever imagined a stone-age nomad, even a well-armed one, could be. *Is this it?* He thought desperately. *This is how I die? At the hands of an African savage?*

The leader pulled the trigger. The Iron Wolfe misfired, sending an electrical current up his arm before catching on fire. He dropped it and yowled.

Gunter heaved a breath of grateful disbelief, a thin laugh escaping. *Saved by your own incompetence*, rang Hiram's authoritative brogue in his head.

Oskar, imperturbable, shot him a contemptuous look and drew his rifle, aiming it at the leader. The rest of the soldiers followed suit.

"We see no need for bloodshed," Oskar said calmly. "But if you fire again, we will wipe this village out."

After a moment's hesitation, the leader put his hands in the air.

"Wise choice," said Oskar.

"We are looking for a metal object about this big. A rotating sphere," Gunter blurted, gesturing with his hands.

The Maasai exchanged glances.

"I'm afraid Sankei has given me some bad news, Herr Doktor," said Oskar.

****

Ravi frowned doubtfully as the airship gained altitude. The hulls, patched with mismatched linen, were thin enough to reveal the patched gas bladders inside. He winced as Hiram turned the knobs on the wireless, resulting in nothing but a static-filled, high-pitched whine.

"Damnable scrap pile," Hiram muttered.

Ravi shook his head. "This will not end well," he said.

"You're a ray of joyous sunshine. Has anyone ever told you that?" said Hiram.

"I can hear leaks," said Ravi. "This airship is leaking."

"It's a fundamental physical property of hydrogen. It's always leaking," returned Hiram.

"That is not very reassuring," said Ravi.

"And I suppose you'd prefer it back on the ground, on the receiving end of the Maasai spears and that Wolfe's Bane contraption?"

"Will you two please stop?" shouted Sophia. "I've had enough of your bickering. We're committed to action, now, what good is second guessing ourselves?"

Ravi shrugged. He peered over the edge at the retreating savannah, the acacia trees becoming like tiny florets in the distance. Ravi could not say when they moved from British territory to German. The savannah was unchanged. The land, peaceably oblivious to the lines drawn by nation-states, made no distinction between German and British, Indian and Maasai.

How many people had seen an aerial view of equatorial Africa? Not many, Ravi warranted. If he was going to die, at least he would do so having seen this.

"Ha! There, in the distance, you see?" said Hiram, handing Ravi the spyglass.

Ravi lifted it, seeing what looked like an enormous pile of kindling. He squinted, making out a small shape on top, which after a moment, he understood was the rocket. The size of the craft implied they were further away than Ravi had at first judged, and he adjusted his mental picture accordingly. It was a very large wood pile, indeed.

"What in the world is that structure?" he asked.

"That," spat Hiram, "is Gunter Wolfe's idea of a launch platform."

"Oh, dear," said Ravi.

"Indeed," Hiram replied. "Good thing it will never be put to the test," he said. He pulled down his brass goggles with a bout of maniacal laughter.

Sophia handed Ravi a knotted rope.

"What's this for?" he asked.

"Safety harness," she said, shimmying into a makeshift one of her own.

"I'm sure it will indeed ensure our safety," Ravi said wryly.

Hiram slapped him on the back. "You wouldn't miss this for the world," he said with a wink.

No, Ravi realized. *I suppose I wouldn't.*

The launch platform came closer. Ravi could see several men, like toy soldiers, pointing upward.

Sophia took the spyglass from Ravi and leaned over the edge.

"Hm. They see us," said Sophia. "I'm not sure, but I think they have guns."

Ravi saw a flash of light from the ground, and a second later, the spyglass was ripped from Sophia's hand.

"They definitely have guns," she said. She grabbed a makeshift handhold nailed to the deck. Ravi hastily followed suit.

A bullet hit one of the airship's many engines, which sputtered and died. Ravi gritted his teeth, ducking behind a sandbag.

Hiram kicked a release behind his podium. The pulley system connected to it went slack, the rope spinning fast enough to send the back end of the ship plummeting. Crates that had held repair materials, now full of ballast, slid toward the stern.

Ravi screamed, realizing that Sophia was screaming in unison. The deck went vertical. They slammed into it as it came to a stop, hanging almost perpendicular to the twin hulls above.

Hiram laughed in a manner that convinced Ravi beyond a shadow of a doubt that he had been truthful to Legishon about his madness. Still laughing, he scrambled onto a podium, connected by ropes to the control surfaces. He perched there like a gargoyle on the steeple of a gothic church.

Ravi watched as the launch pad barreled toward them. *If the Bedlam has miscalculated, I am soon to be smashed into paste,* he thought wildly.

The ship was brought up short as it enveloped the rocket. Hiram turned the engines around to halt its forward movement.

Ravi's heart bucked and shuddered like a spooked horse. He breathed a jagged sigh of relief.

"What are you waiting for? Now!" Hiram yelled.

Spurred to action, Ravi and Sophia threw chains back and forth from opposite sides of the deck, attaching them around the rocket.

In the mayhem, Ravi had not noticed horse hooves thundering toward them until he heard a familiar voice.

"Damn you, Codon!" screamed Gunter Wolfe.

Ravi doubled his efforts. He had never thought himself afraid of Gunter, but hearing his voice now made his already pounding heart want to crash through his ribcage in an attempt to flee.

"Stop them!" Gunter yelled.

A shot rang out. As tempted as he was to dive for cover, Ravi kept his mind on his task, knowing that the best way to get out of here alive was to finish.

"Don't shoot at them, you fool! The whole thing could explode!" yelled Gunter.

Ravi looked down and saw the soldiers swarming the airship, wicked knives drawn.

"Oh, no," Ravi muttered, sorry he'd looked.

He and Sophia, still suspended on ropes, zipped down the deck, tightening the lines around the rocket.

Hiram grunted, turning a hand-crank to pull the stern level.

"Will you two get back here and help me with this!" he yelled.

Ravi looked down, still half-hanging from the rope. "How?" he yelled in return.

Hiram, not quite strong enough to pull the ship back into position, watched helplessly as the stern bumped into the launch platform.

Already off balance from the chains holding it, the rocket teetered precariously before falling forward. Ravi cried out as the airship lurched down and forward, almost bouncing off the ground.

Momentarily airborne, Ravi scrambled to regain his footing. He couldn't. He freefell, his organs lurching as he dropped. *This is it*, he cringed, as the platform rose to meet him. His body tensed with anticipation of impact.

With an unpleasant yank under his arms, he remembered the safety harness. He dangled eight feet off the ground. *Sophia, I could kiss you,* he thought.

Hiram turned the airship's engines to push them upward faster.

Ravi, dangling helplessly, glanced up at Sophia, who attempted to re-secure the rocket on her own.

He yowled as something yanked his leg. He looked down to see Gunter, with a savage expression, trying to claw his way up Ravi and onto the airship. Ravi kicked at him.

The airship bobbed along the ground with the rocket skimming the dirt. Soldiers scattered to avoid being run down.

"We're too heavy! Push the ballast over!" Hiram yelled.

Ravi watched as Sophia threw everything she could reach over the side. Food, chains, boxes, anything not bolted down.

The airship rose. The ground receded beneath Ravi, Gunter still clutching his legs.

Suddenly, something pounded Ravi in the gut. He fought back a wave of nausea, but whatever it was knocked Gunter loose. He hurled through the air and then slammed into the dirt on his back with a thud. Ravi glanced up to Sophia, who was grinning as she continued to toss objects down at Gunter.

Ravi, however grateful at not having Gunter's extra weight pulling him down, still hung limply over the side. His underarms were rubbed raw and screaming with pain.

He felt himself rising as Sophia and Hiram pulled him up on deck. Hiram gestured obscenely to Gunter, still laughing like a madman.

Once on deck, Ravi patted himself down. *No harm done,* he thought, *other than a little rope burn.* Then his head swam and he sank to a seated position.

Sophia handed Ravi a flask of water. "Drink this," she said.

Hiram waved his hat in the air. "Well done, lads!" He said.

Sophia glared at him.

"Oh, and lady, of course," he said with an eye roll. "You are still wearing Mukherjee's trousers. But well done, anyway! Nothing can stop us, now!"

"I hate it when you say that," said Ravi.

"Nonsense," said Hiram, grabbing the radio receiver.

Again, the crackle of static and a high-pitched whir filled the air, setting Ravi's teeth on edge.

"Now that there is no more interference with the wireless..." Hiram began. Ravi was about to protest when the line became clear. He said nothing, stunned to silence at something on this airship working properly.

"Codon to Rhodes," said Hiram. "Are you there, sir?"

The tinny sound of Rhodes' voice crackled through the wireless. "Why yes, Hiram, as a matter of fact I am," he said. Ravi could tell instantly that something was wrong. The tone of Rhodes' voice was too cheerful.

"And I've got a visitor. Major, say hello to Mister Codon," said Rhodes.

13

Chapter

Sophia's expression changed rapidly from shock, to horror, to chagrin. Ravi and Hiram exchanged glances.

"Codon, you've crossed the line..." came the voice of Major Westbridge.

Rhodes' voice cut back in. "Imagine my surprise when I heard that Major Westbridge was here to see me. I thought, two Major Westbridges in one day, well isn't that odd?"

Sophia blushed. Even Hiram looked sheepish.

"I believe my Major Westbridge has something he'd like to say to you," said Rhodes.

"My daughter had better be in one piece, you wretched mountebank!" The static picked up on the wireless again, as if the Major's anger could come through in the form of a lightning bolt. "Sophia! Are you there?"

"I'm here, father," she said sheepishly, removing the pith helmet. Her honey-colored curls tumbled out, framing her very young, pixie-like face.

"Good. Thank God you're safe," said Westbridge. "Now, we're going back to England, and you will marry and settle down like a proper lady."

"Marry? Who, father?" Sophia demanded.

"There are plenty of young men from which to choose."

"But I don't want..." Sophia began.

"I have had enough of your insolence, young lady. Now put Codon on the line!"

"You might be over-reacting just a tad, Major," said Hiram, taking the microphone from Sophia.

"Over-reacting? I am the very model of restraint! You'll bring my daughter back here this instant!" shouted Westbridge. "And if you ever come within fifty feet of me or my daughter again I'll have you jailed!"

Ravi winced.

"Fly that airship of yours to Salisbury," said Rhodes. "I'll be there in two days to determine the future of your project."

"Thank you, sir," said Hiram.

"Don't thank me, you presumptuous lout," said Rhodes. "Did you really plan to send a lady up in that rocket ship of yours? And the Major tells me that the craft requires two pilots. Your second seat would be occupied by whom, I might ask? Yourself, risking the entire program's future?"

"Sir, I've found that Mister Mukherjee is well adept..." Hiram began.

"Your manservant?" Rhodes said incredulously. "Really, Mister Codon. You must return at once. We must put this adventure of yours on hold until we can complete the project in a professional manner worthy of the British South Africa Company name, not to mention the reputation of the Crown."

This was too much for Ravi. He reached out and yanked one of the antennae.

"I hope... myself clear," said Rhodes, his voice now full of static.

Ravi pushed the other antennae and started randomly turning knobs.

"Mister Rhodes? You are breaking up, sir," said Hiram.

Static and feedback erupted through the speaker. Ravi hoped Rhodes found it every bit as annoying as he did.

Some garbled voices came through amid the static.

"Please repeat, I didn't get that last," said Hiram.

"...my words... harm to my daughter... have you tarred and made into a masthead... " came Westbridge's voice. Ravi stomped over to the machine and turned it off.

Hiram looked up at Ravi in surprise.

"We can launch," said Ravi. "Right now."

Hiram, for once in his life, fell silent.

"Well?" said Ravi.

"It's one thing to cut off that blatherhound Rhodes on the wireless," said Hiram. "It's quite another to openly defy the Crown."

"I knew it!" shouted Ravi. "You claim to be so independent, oh, I'm not British I'm Irish, I go wherever I please and invent whatever I want. But when it comes down to it, you'll do exactly as you're told."

Ravi paced the deck angrily, deeply disappointed in Hiram. *Why?* He thought. *My career was made doing things the appropriate way.* And look where that had gotten him. The realization hit him with a near physical impact. No pioneer ever did things the way they had always been done. He looked to Sophia to back him up, but she sat sulking, eyes downcast.

"We have the capability. Do you want the credit for inventing the thing, or do you want Rhodes to give the project to someone else to finish? Someone who will undoubtedly take credit for your work?"

"You of all people understand that you need resources in order to build things!" said Hiram.

"Am I wrong that the thing is built already? That the Germans went so far as to fuel it in preparation to launch? We have everything we need to make the launch right here. Right now."

Hiram looked up, doubtfully. "Provided we can fix the damage caused by those bloody Huns trying to stop us."

"Then we should get to work. What damage should I be looking for?"

Hiram tentatively rose. "Very small things. Also, you two have no aeronautical expertise. If you go up in that cockpit, you will both have to do exactly what I say, can you do that?"

Ravi turned to Sophia, who still looked glum. She wore the same expression of guilt she had that first night on the airship.

"Sophia, what do you say?" He said to her gently. "Are you still curious about what it's like to pilot the flying machine? Do you still want to be the first to see the world as it appears from space?"

She made eye contact with him, breaking into a broad grin. "The British Navy wants a Westbridge in the cockpit, and they will get one," she said.

Ravi turned to Hiram. "If you can make this machine fly, we can take it to the Moon if you tell us the way," he said.

"God willing, someday we shall do just that."

"Could we perhaps fly over the ocean in order to avoid being shot at in territorial disputes?"

Hiram angled the engines to gain altitude at maximum speed.

****

The patched and battered airship flew several miles off the African coast, rising into the wispy clouds. Ravi leaned over the side, watching a school of dolphins leaping.

"Beautiful, aren't they?" Sophia said, breathlessly.

Ravi agreed.

"Made more beautiful by the fact that they don't have guns," said Hiram, patting her on the shoulder.

Ravi squinted into the hazy horizon and then lifted the eyeglass. A Majestic Class Battleship of the British Royal Navy came into focus.

"No, but I'm sure they do," said Ravi.

Hiram peered through the glass. "Ha! Don't worry, it's one of ours."

"You forget," said Ravi, "that we are now openly disobeying orders."

"Ah, yes, but they don't know that," Hiram said. "They don't have a wireless! All they know is that we've got a Union Jack and so do they."

Ravi gave Hiram a dubious look. As reasonable as that sounded, luck had not been with them on this journey.

Hiram ducked back into the rocket to finish his task.

"Of all the execrable..." he muttered. Forgetting he was inside the rocket, he tried to stand and smacked his head on some ill-placed apparatus. He howled in pain.

"Mukherjee, give me a hand here."

"Is something wrong?" Ravi asked.

Hiram pointed at the open panel.

A bullet had punctured a brass pump connected to the fuel lines.

Ravi's heart sank. "I see. That powers the pump to pressurize the fuel tanks if I'm not mistaken?"

"No, Mukherjee, you are not mistaken. You are also not flying into the outer void today, thanks to the ineptitude of the good Doctor Wolfe."

"We can fix it, right? You built this machine, surely you can fix it?" said Sophia, her giddy excitement evaporating, replaced by apprehension.

Hiram glowered. "Do you have a finely crafted mesh of sodium permanganate and an acetylene torch about your person, Miss Westbridge?"

Sophia glowered right back. "Can't we improvise? We should be able to come by some sort of torch..."

"I'm afraid I am all out of chewing gum and nail files with which to fix it, Miss Westbridge," Hiram said wryly.

"Well, there has to be something," said Sophia.

"I suppose we could summon a djinn, who may procure a flying carpet for us," said Hiram.

"Hush, Sophia is right," said Ravi. "We must improvise. Is there enough initial pressure in the tanks to start the engine?"

"Yes, but it won't last more than a second or two without the pump."

"Does it have to run outside the atmosphere?" Ravi asked.

Hiram huffed. "Oh, for a few seconds, the upper stage is entirely undamaged. But without the steam generator to run the pump it's a moot point." He enunciated this carefully, looking Ravi in the eye as if he were being simple.

Ravi returned his gaze. "Then all we need is another power source to drive the pump."

Hiram threw up his hands. "Yes, which will take weeks to fabricate," he growled.

"Outside the envelope, Mister Codon," he said, patting Hiram on the shoulder like he was so fond of doing to Ravi and Sophia. He turned to the propeller on the airship's disabled engine as it slowly spun in the wind. "I have an idea," he said.

Hiram squinted at the propeller, then back at Ravi. "You don't mean," he began. He paced, his face locked in a skeptical grimace as he mulled it over. Then, suddenly, he looked at Ravi as if he'd never seen him before. "By the beard of Zeus! That might actually work!"

Ravi smiled. "I believe it will," he said.

"Of course, it might cut out at an inopportune moment and send you and Miss Westbridge plummeting unceremoniously into the ocean," Hiram finished.

"So, what has changed?" Ravi said wryly.

"Ha, ha!" said Hiram. "I'm willing to give it a go if you are."

Ravi pulled on a pair of goggles much like Hiram's, and the two of them set to work removing the propeller from the dead engine. They worked through the rest of the day and on into the evening before succumbing to exhaustion and the darkness of a night over the ocean. All the while they travelled northeast, taking them to the launch area Hiram had selected. The craft had been designed for a single orbit of the earth; launching from too far out at sea or too near unfriendly territory would not allow for a safe landing. Launching near southern India had the additional advantage of being nearly equatorial, allowing the rocket to take maximum advantage of the Earth's own rotation.

As the sun crept up from the horizon, Hiram lowered their improvised fuel pump assembly to the rocket via the complex pulley system, while Ravi cobbled together an array of tubes and gears which would enable the pump to be driven by the propeller.

The wind whipped through Ravi's hair as he tightened bolts into place. The makeshift propeller system marred the rocket's smooth lines. Still, the sight of the propeller spinning lazily in the front of the craft like his Penaud toy helicopter sent a thrill of wonder through him.

From the top of the rocket, he leaned down to look inside. Sophia examined valves, pressure gauges, and levers comparing them to Hiram's hand-written diagrams. She had fastened leather pads to all the sharp edges in a cursory attempt at a safety precaution. Ravi fought back the urge to make fun of them, since one of her crude safety devices had somehow saved his life.

She turned to him with a radiant grin. "Exciting, isn't it?" she breathed.

"Indeed," he replied, dropping down to the deck.

Hiram sauntered over, examining Ravi's work. "Magnificent!" he said.

Ravi beamed.

"Adequate, at any rate," said Hiram. Ravi's look faded to one of annoyance.

"Go on, get inside," Hiram continued. "The air is getting thin, and we're only going to ascend from here."

Only when Ravi had crawled into the capsule next to Sophia did he realize how small it truly was. Inside the cramped space, there was no way to avoid their legs touching. Intensely aware of the smell of her skin, and the small amount of perfume she must have carried all the way to Africa and back again, he found it difficult to stay on task.

Ravi jolted upright as Hiram pounded on the window. Wearing an oxygen mask and goggles, he grinned broadly, giving them the thumbs up.

"I kind of like the eccentric old coot," said Sophia.

A shadow fell across Hiram that Ravi hoped was a large cloud. Hiram looked up with an expression that suggested it was not. He ran out of view, Ravi twisting inside the capsule to try to see what was happening outside.

"What's going on?" Sophia asked, her voice apprehensive. "Should we get out?"

Before Ravi could respond, the hatch opened, and a towering figure moved into view, silhouetted against the clear sky.

"Get out!" it screamed. "Schnell!"

Chapter

A meaty hand roughly grabbed Ravi's forearm. Ravi tore free from its grip and stepped out, adjusting his jacket and tie. "I'll thank you to keep your hands off me," he said.

Another airship, half the size of Hiram's, but better equipped, hovered directly above them. It bore the Iron Cross, Imperial German markings. Ropes dangled to the deck from above.

A soldier stuffed the barrel of Gunter's lightning gun, which Hiram had referred to as the 'Wolfe's Bane,' into Ravi's face. The first soldier, who appeared to be in command, was manhandling Sophia.

"Stay still!" he growled.

Sophia sprang from the cockpit like an angry cat and whirled on him. "Which is it? Get out or stay still? You'll need to choose one, you know."

"Now that you are out," said the commander, "Stay still." He turned, barked something in German at the soldier, and stepped into the rocket.

The soldier stood menacingly between Ravi and the rocket, pushing the Wolfe's Bane into his chest. He stepped forward, pushing them toward the bow.

"Now what?" Sophia whispered in his ear.

Now what, indeed, he thought.

"What's our plan?" she prompted, again.

Ravi was not a soldier, and he was unaccustomed to people aiming large weapons at him, experimental or not, at point blank range. While he was indeed a planner, this was not the kind of plan at which he was adept.

"No talking!" The soldier yelled.

Sophia glared at him, and then turned back to Ravi as if waiting for a response to what she clearly thought was a reasonable query.

Still at a loss, he was ready to say so when he noticed that the Wolfe's Bane's power cell was loose, exposing the leads. He looked pointedly at Sophia, trying to catch her eye, and then glanced at the exposed leads. As he had hoped, her eyes followed. She nodded slightly, comprehending. The soldier looked back and forth between the two. Ravi smiled pleasantly.

"Surely you need not feel threatened by the lady and me," he said. "Such a copious display of force is unnecessary."

The soldier blinked in incomprehension, shoving the barrel of the weapon into his chest, yet again. *That is becoming tedious*, he thought.

"Do you speak English?" Ravi asked.

"No talking!" the soldier yelled again.

"Oh, for the love of..." Sophia began. The soldier glared menacingly, as if torn about whether to shove the weapon at a lady.

"Don't you dare, you ill-mannered thug!" Ravi said.

"More! Try to make him angry," Sophia whispered.

"I can't very well taunt him if he doesn't understand what I'm saying," said Ravi.

"Very well, I can," said Sophia, stepping toward the soldier.

"Sophia, no!" Ravi gasped, alarmed.

The soldier turned the weapon on her, eyes wide. "Halt! Sitzen!" he yelled.

Ravi stepped in front of Sophia. Then the distant report of battleship guns filled the air. All three of them paused, listening.

Ravi grabbed Sophia and hit the deck as a deafening blast surrounded them. He heard the alarmed cries from the German airship crew above, and saw that the attacking ship was on fire. *Hiram was right about the battleship crew only noticing the markings*, he thought.

Shrapnel from the explosion hit the gas bladders. Ravi hauled Sophia to her feet and they made a break for the rear deck.

The soldier yelled after them. "Halt! Halt!"

Ravi heard the soldier fire. He leapt into the air, taking Sophia with him. He felt the lightning bolt singe his pant leg, the static electricity jolting his calf. He whirled, watching as the weapon discharged electricity through the weak seal on the power cell. The lightning hit a chain secured to the deck. He grabbed Sophia's hand and peered around to make sure he wasn't touching anything metallic. He turned toward the stern, suddenly worried about Hiram.

Meanwhile, the soldier convulsed violently, crashing to the deck and dropping the weapon. His eyes rolled back, a gurgling noise escaped his throat. Finally, he stopped shaking, passed out, a thin line of drool gathering on the deck.

****

As Hiram watched Gunter approach, accompanied by an armed soldier, he was a little bit hurt, but also a little bit flattered that his old partner thought it necessary to bring along minions with weapons in order to steal his work. *Though he's carrying that malfunctioning contraption of Gunter's instead of a proper sidearm,* he thought. *I may gain the upper hand, yet.*

It was also clear that Gunter was quite angry. So angry, in fact, he was losing some of his smugness. And that meant he would soon be losing his calm facade. Hiram did not intend to miss his opening, though truth be told, he was having a difficult time maintaining his own composure.

"You're slipping, Gunter," said Hiram.

"The release sequence you old fool! Now!" Gunter yelled, red-faced.

"Listen to me," growled Hiram. "This machine is—"

"Mine. I'll make it work without you if I have to," said Gunter, as if it were a threat. "But I prefer efficiency."

"Then step off my bloody deck," said Hiram, through gritted teeth.

Gunter flushed, grabbing one of the chains connecting the hulls to the deck. His knuckles were white. "I designed the combustion chamber! The refinery! Perfected the fuel mixture! This is my rocket!" he shouted.

"Built to my specifications. My design with my money," said Hiram. "You are a hired plumber, Mister Wolfe, and I will not have you blundering about—"

"Shut up!" yelled Gunter.

Then he jolted, pulling his hand away from the chain. He looked down at the mild electrical burn on his palm. "What the..." he muttered.

Hiram grinned. Gunter looked up just in time to see Hiram's fist flying toward his face.

****

"We need to get him out of the rocket," Sophia whispered.

"Why do you keep looking at me to figure everything out?" Ravi whispered back.

"Because you're good at it!" she replied.

"So are you," he said.

She blinked. "You think so?" she said, as if he'd complimented her on her hat.

She looked up, deep in thought.

"Okay, then," she said, "here goes."

Sophia rapped on the side of the rocket, out of view.

Ravi gaped, incredulous. "What are you doing?" he whispered. She looked up, grabbing a ballast bag tied to the rigging above.

"He's not going to fall for that," Ravi whispered, but he moved to help her.

The German commander irritably stood to find the source of the interruption. Sophia and Ravi swung the ballast bag as hard as they could.

It slammed into the commander's face. He blinked in confusion a few times and then collapsed in a heap. Sophia and Ravi pulled him out of the rocket.

Ravi peered toward the stern just in time to see the other soldier bludgeoning Hiram with Wolfe's Bane.

He grabbed Sophia's arm. They ran.

"No!" He heard Hiram yell. "Get back inside!"

The soldier knocked Hiram down.

"You get in, I'll go," said Ravi.

Reluctantly, she darted back to the rocket.

Ravi bull-rushed the German soldier. While this had the desired effect of stopping him from bludgeoning Hiram, it had the less desired effect of catching his attention. The soldier wheeled on Ravi, slamming him down on the deck. While it was not the most painful thing that had happened on this journey so far, it was far from pleasant. *I should have spent more time fighting as a boy*, he chided himself.

Hiram and Gunter faced off, Hiram with his fists up in English boxing style.

Ravi dragged himself to his feet, ready to lose this fight in hopes that Hiram would win his and then do something to help. Suddenly a ballast bag on a rope swung into the soldier, knocking him clear off the side of the airship.

Ravi peered back toward the bow, seeing Sophia standing in the spacecraft's open hatch. She waved and dropped back inside.

Ravi's broad smile faded as he saw the German commander getting up and climbing onto the rocket. Ravi ran. *I don't think I'm going to make it*, he thought wildly.

He grabbed one of the dangling ropes and kicked out in front. His stomach dipped, and if he had eaten anything that day, he would have been in danger of vomiting.

He had just been thinking of getting to Sophia before the German, but since the opportunity presented itself, he straightened his legs and kicked the commander in the chest. The German flew back six feet and scrambled at the edge of the deck, falling into the rigging.

Ravi leapt on top of the rocket. He saw Gunter turn from Hiram and bolt toward him. Ravi dropped down into the carriage next to Sophia.

"Are we going?" she asked.

Ravi slammed the hatch closed and turned the lock wheel as fast as he could to seal it.

"I have no idea," he said.

The lock wheel, however, had other ideas. It became more and more difficult to turn until it stubbornly insisted on turning the other way. *This is embarrassing*, he thought.

"A little help," he said. Sophia reached up and turned.

Something large thumped against the top of the rocket. Sophia jumped.

"What was that?" she asked.

"I suspect it was Doctor Wolfe," said Ravi.

Sophia made a strangled sound. "He's fighting us!" She said.

"Is this news?" asked Ravi.

"No, I mean with the hatch," she said.

"I know," Ravi said. "He almost has it open,"

Then the tail end of the rocket dropped suddenly, leaving them hanging and pointed at the sky.

****

Hiram, both bloody and bloody angry, got up and limped to the console. He figured his nose was broken. His ankle would be tender for a while. Who knew the scrawny bastard had it in him?

But Gunter Wolfe was doomed to lose. Why? Because he simply didn't know what he was doing.

Hiram grabbed a lever connected to a chain running to a series of pulleys. He yanked it back with a grunt.

Take that, you Teutonic gargoyle, he thought.

Profoundly satisfied, Hiram watched the back end of the rocket drop, sending Gunter plummeting behind. Gunter dangled from the locking mechanism. Ravi and Sophia, visible through the open hatch, both screamed, struggling with Gunter to pull the top closed.

Also screaming was Oskar von Rauch, who scrambled to grab chains, no longer attached to the ship, in a desperate and failing attempt to prevent his untimely death.

Hiram admired the rocket for a moment, and then reached for another lever.

A surge of guilt made him hesitate. After a few seconds, he called out to his former partner. "Gunter!"

Gunter looked up, still hostile, still clinging to the rocket.

"Grab that rope," said Hiram, pointing.

Many ropes and chains now dangled near the rocket, but fortunately for Gunter, the one he needed was the closest. He tentatively reached out with one hand, still clinging to the rocket with the other.

Ravi's arm reached out, slamming the hatch shut. Gunter scrambled for it, still holding the rope, but the lock mechanism spun and clicked into place.

Fair warning, thought Hiram, pulling the lever to release the forward lock. The rocket fell. So did Gunter. He grabbed the rope with both hands.

The rocket trailed a wire, unspooling until it pulled free and ignited the engine. Hiram, lightheaded with elation, watched as the rocket streaked through the sky. An almost clear flame spewed from the back like a glassblowing torch while the propeller spun madly on the front.

Hiram's eyes followed the rocket until it was only a tiny point of light glinting in the sky. Flushed with pride, he turned, looking for someone to share his triumph.

His smile faded and his shoulders slumped as he saw only a bedraggled Gunter, glumly hauling himself onto the deck. Hiram locked eyes with the remaining German soldier, who looked dazed and a little the worse for wear. The man hurled the lightning gun over the side of the airship and raised both hands.

Chapter

Ravi closed his eyes and gritted his teeth against the crushing acceleration, feeling as if the rocket were a rampaging elephant and all he could do was cling for dear life. The velocity dropped as suddenly as it started. Ravi lurched forward in his seat. He breathed deeply, trying to settle his stomach.

It would not do to vomit in an enclosed space, he told himself. *Especially in front of a lady.* Once again, he was grateful for the sparse rations.

"Is—is that it?" Sophia asked, her voice trembling slightly.

Ravi opened his eyes. A black sky framed the horizon. The earth shone with a bright blue hazy aura, like a halo, beneath them. *Beneath them!*

His breath caught in his throat. He thought of the devas in their magnificent vimanas, coming down to Earth from impossibly far away. He was seeing something no human in recorded history had seen.

"Is it," Sophia pressed, "I thought there was supposed to be..."

Without warning, Ravi was slammed back against the seat with a grunt. His head hit the leather cushion Sophia had attached to it, and once again he was grateful for her foresight.

Sophia began to giggle. He turned his head, peering at her with one open eye. Tears streamed down her cheeks as she gasped with breathy laughter. *Oh, dear,* thought Ravi. *I do hope she doesn't lose her mind.*

Out of the viewport, Ravi saw the propeller apparatus fall away. Hiram had explained this would happen, though he was a bit sad to see it go after so much work.

The second stage engine stopped. Stillness.

Ravi and Sophia hung over the earth like a pair of mad trapeze artists tangled in an impossible contortion.

"Ravi, look," Sophia breathed. He was glad she had stopped giggling and was restored to speech.

They could see all of India beneath them. Africa, too.

"The cartographers did a fairly decent job, considering," Ravi mused.

Sophia giggled again. This time, she noticed his alarmed look, however, and stopped. "It's just... a bit like an angel showing up for tea," she said.

He smiled at her and took her hand. She smiled, and then gasped.

"The latch," she said.

"What? Of course," he said, pulling a lever. A dull clang of a metal latch releasing, vibrating through the tiny craft, was the only sound as Ravi watched the spent rocket leisurely float away in the little round mirror mounted in the viewport frame.

A crackling of radio static filled the cabin.

"What do you see?" came Hiram's voice, as if through a tin can. "Are you taking photographs?"

Sophia, now reminded, fumbled with the Kodak Number One camera mounted by her window.

"Yes," said Ravi, into the transceiver microphone. "Everything is fine."

"Be sure to get a photo of the spent rocket stage," said Hiram excitedly. "It's the first man-made satellite."

The second stage, falling away rapidly, appeared only about the size of his palm. Sophia winced and turned the camera toward it.

"It's broadcasting. I can hear it on the wireless. Wonderful!" Hiram gushed. He'd installed a battery-powered wireless set in the second stage which was at that moment broadcasting for anyone who might by some chance possess the right equipment and happen to tune to it as it passed over.

Sophia snapped photos of the diminishing second stage.

"Mukherjee, don't forget my samples! I need to see about this aether business, once and for all. Whether it exists and, if so, what it's made of!"

"I wonder if the wireless is such a great idea," murmured Ravi. "Hiram somehow manages to be annoying from very far away."

Ravi loaded a sample jar into a small airlock fitted with a complex mechanism for securing, opening and resealing it.

"You'll be over the horizon, soon. Be sure to..."

Hiram's voice disintegrated into static as Australia came into view.

Ravi felt a stab of fear when Hiram cut out, despite the fact that he had just now been complaining about him. He and Sophia were now well and truly alone. With no chatter on the wireless, the silence of space engulfed them. He busied himself with the sample jars as Sophia snapped photos.

"Is that Tchaikovsky you're humming?" Sophia asked.

"What?"

"Tchaikovsky. The 1812 Overture."

"Was I? Sorry. It's... awfully quiet out here," said Ravi.

"Yes, and it will be dark soon, too," she replied. They would soon move behind the earth, where it was now night.

As they rounded the curvature of the earth, the first thing they saw was the moon, like a frozen lake reflecting firelight.

"I see why the ancients thought the moon a goddess," Sophia said. Ravi could see its reflection in her eyes. A stray curl fell into her face. Shyly, he brushed it back behind her ear. She looked for a moment like she would like him to kiss her, and he would have, if it hadn't been for the limited range of movement in the capsule. Then, the moment passed and her eyes moved again to the viewport.

"Who knew there would be so many lights?" she exclaimed. Though the shape of North America was not easily visible in the darkness, clusters of lights pinpointed the cities. "Some are like fireflies and some like lightning bugs. Could it be the difference between gas and electric lights?"

"Quite so," said Ravi.

"I wonder if we are flying over Thomas Edison and Nikola Tesla right now. I wonder if they are looking back at us," she said.

"I doubt anyone could even see us. We're probably nothing more than a speck," said Ravi.

A dogsledder, traveling across the Canadian tundra, stopped to watch a star streaking across the night sky.

On an ocean liner in the north Atlantic, a group of passengers marveled at the strange flashing light. A small boy, obsessed with The War of the Worlds, sped across the ship to warn everyone about the Martian invasion.

On the balcony of Buckingham palace, Queen Victoria and several attendants gazed at the point of light making its way steadily across the horizon.

In Istanbul, several Muslims stopped in mid-prayer, gaping at the bright light passing over the sky, framed by minarets.

At the helm, Hiram ran the radio with one hand, flying the battered airship with the other. The radio emitted a series of beeps, signifying that his spacecraft had nearly completed its orbit. He was grateful for the noise and also the multitasking, which were keeping him awake.

Gunter seemed to be taking some small satisfaction in not helping him, which only bothered him insofar as he had lost several pounds on this trip and he would have very much liked to hike up his pants, maybe adjust his belt.

The airship leaked badly, some of the bladders noticeably sagging. They were losing altitude. Part of the canvas covering had torn loose and flapped in the wind. This would be the last voyage for this dear ship, which, it occurred to him, he had never bothered to name. He hadn't named the rocket either, but it would be prudent to work in Cecil Rhodes somehow, assuming the landing went as intended. If not, then it would be called Codon's End. But every moment that passed increased their chances of success.

The rigging above Hiram groaned heavily. A high pitched shout cut through the radio. Hiram winced. The German soldier jolted awake and threw his hands in the air. Gunter muttered something under his breath.

"Mister Codon? Can you hear me?" came Mukherjee's voice through the radio. Hiram nearly leapt with glee.

"Yes, of course, my good man," said Hiram. "You're ready to come down to Earth, I take it?"

Yes, thought Ravi, *and no*.

"If I'm reading this gage correctly," said Ravi, "we have only one hour of air left. Please do tell me I am mistaken."

After a moment of silence, Hiram said, "No need for worry, you'll be back well before then."

Ravi turned to Sophia. "He's reassuring us again," he said.

"Oh, no," she said, suddenly apprehensive.

They both turned to the handwritten sheet of paper with Hiram's landing instructions tacked to the console. Step one was explained with a series of diagrams that Ravi and Sophia both found somewhat perplexing.

"Lock the reentry sighting apparatus into place," said Hiram.

Ravi looked over the mass of armatures, gages and valves around him before pulling on an articulated arm with several lenses securely housed at the end. Each lens was etched with a complex pattern of arcs and crosshairs, ending with a mirror mounted at a fory-five degree angle. The arm locked in place. The mirror reflected the crescent of the Earth through the array of lenses.

The apparatus had clearly been intended for a somewhat taller man. Ravi needed to sit tall and inch up in the pilot's seat in order for the lens patterns to line up with each other. He knew that the combined pattern was supposed to line up exactly with the horizon.

It didn't.

"Now what," he murmured.

"It says to fire thrusters to adjust reentry angle," Sophia said.

"Right," he said.

Ravi nervously placed two fingers on the polished wood ball that topped the four-way maneuvering control to his right. Still straining to keep his eye line with the lenses, he nudged the lever, opening a series of valves. The rocket emitted jets of air, crystallizing into glittering mist. The craft gently turned.

"Be gentle with the thrusters. It doesn't take much," Hiram barked.

"Working on it," Sophia said quickly.

The Earth was moving entirely out of view as the craft turned. Ravi tried to suppress a sick look, and knew he was unsuccessful when Sophia blurted out, "What is it? What's wrong?"

"Don't panic!" said Hiram. "It only takes a little nudge."

Ravi tapped the maneuvering control. A hiss of compressed air escaped and the view through the window began to shift back toward the Earth, now rotated a quarter turn.

They watched as jets of air sprayed out of the craft in short bursts, turning it this way and that. Each jet froze into a fountain of tiny ice crystals like a glittering halo.

Ravi sighed in frustration, tapping the controls, first one way, and then the other.

"You're overcompensating. I can hear your teeth grinding all the way down here," Hiram barked. "Relax."

"Yes, being in a wooden box thousands of miles above the earth is as relaxing as afternoon tea," muttered Ravi.

But he was starting to get a feel for it. He gently tapped the control for brief bursts, coaxing rather than forcing the craft.

After what seemed an exceedingly long and stressful battle with the little device, Ravi had the arc of the Earth lined up in his glass instruments. The curvature was very slightly off, as though the Earth were marginally larger than the etching suggested, or their altitude was not as high as Hiram had intended.

"We are ready," Ravi said as confidently as he could manage. Sophia tried to peer over his shoulder to check, but was unable to get the right viewing angle through the numerous lenses.

"I've done all the calculations," Hiram replied. "Just aim for central India."

Sophia worked a crank, extending a second mirror outside the craft. It took up half of Ravi's view through the window, reflecting the Earth's surface below.

They were directly over ocean.

"The crosshairs mark your landing site at the moment you fire the reentry thrusters," Hiram said. "It's angled to compensate for your speed and altitude, within a few dozen miles," he added quickly. A moment passed. "Timing is crucial, lad."

India was drifting into view beneath them, though slightly off if the etched guidelines were to be trusted.

Ravi took a deep breath. The craft was no more delicate than the clockwork lion he had disassembled and reassembled as a young boy. Those mechanical components were so small he'd needed tweezers and a monocle to put it back together, but put it together he did. And it worked. Surely he could make this slight adjustment. Just a hair's breadth...

Through the eyepiece, the reticule remained lined up with the horizon and the crosshairs were dead center over India.

"I have it!" he exclaimed.

"Excelsior!" shouted Hiram.

Ravi heard Sophia's long, slow sigh of relief.

"Now fire the reentry thrusters," said Hiram. "And try not to move around."

Ravi reached up to a series of electric switches overhead, away from everything else.

He flipped them one by one. On the third, a bang like a gunshot jolted them. They locked eyes, terrified.

"That was supposed to happen, right?" Sophia asked.

"I think so. Yes," said Ravi. Several panels from the top of the craft had detached and were now hurling through space away from them. Hiram's drawings showed this, but it was much less terrifying on paper.

"Okay, so we're back in the atmosphere," said Sophia.

With that, Ravi's stomach lurched into his throat as they plummeted toward the earth. The craft buffeted wildly. Ravi saw flames race by through the window.

Now, this cannot possibly be right, Ravi thought as the craft shook violently. "Codon, we're on fire!" he yelled into the wireless, receiving only static by way of response. *Of course it doesn't work, you idiot*, he realized, *we're on fire!*

He could do nothing about the heat ionization, about hurling toward the earth like a stray cannonball, or being engulfed in flames. He doubted he could even die well, though no one would likely notice since Sophia had put her hands over her face, being too preoccupied with her own panic to notice his.

The violent shaking stopped, in favor of a merely excessive bouncing. Ravi peeked out the window. The flames had ceased.

"Oh, thank God, the fire is out," said Sophia, flushed.

"We are still falling very fast," said Ravi.

They each looked at Hiram's chart and reached for the next series of levers.

"Did it work?" Sophia asked.

Suddenly, the craft was jerked up short, descending slowly.

"It appears so," Ravi replied. He knew that Hiram's brightly colored silk parachutes, months of work on the part of seamstresses, had deployed. Though he'd always appreciated a good tailor, his respect for the profession was now on par with that of doctors, since they had indeed saved his life.

There were four parachutes in all, a hodgepodge of whatever colored silks were available, purples, blues, greens and reds. He wondered what they must look like from the ground. *Perhaps like an incense decanter carried by a flock of strange tropical birds,* he mused.

Ravi took a deep breath, certain for the first time since leaving Cecil Rhodes' office that his death was not imminent. He was immediately starving and exhausted, wanting nothing more than to make up for all the lost meals and sleep.

"I think we made it," Sophia said. She also was regaining her composure, looking relieved but also invigorated. "Can you see anything on your side? All I can see is clouds," she said.

Ravi peered through the window. At first he could see nothing, but as they cleared the mist, he began to make out the land beneath them.

"Do you know where we are?" Sophia asked. "Are we in central India? What happens if it's a very remote area and no one is there?"

He saw that there was a river, and that the green was broken up by several structures. It quickly became clear that they were not headed for rolling hills and spacious green, but a populated area, probably one of the larger towns.

"What do you see on your side?" he asked.

"It looks like, well, that can't be right," Sophia began.

Ravi looked questioningly at her.

"I think it's the ocean," she said.

Ravi's heart sank.

"Oh, no," said Ravi.

"What is it?" she asked.

"Why is it," Ravi said, "That whenever anyone says something like 'nothing could possibly go wrong' or 'I think we made it,' it is as if the gods think we are complaining because things aren't difficult enough."

Ravi peered out the window, Kolkata rising up to greet them.

Chapter 16

As they descended, Ravi could see a crowd gathering, pointing up at what must be the strangest thing they had ever seen.

He wished he could steer the craft, at least so that it would land in an empty street. Like so much of this venture, however, he had absolutely no control whatsoever. The cursed thing would land where it would land.

Ravi saw a man dive out of the way. Then they heard a loud crunch beneath them. Ravi grabbed Sophia's hand as the spacecraft rolled, sending Ravi sliding unceremoniously into Sophia, pinning her against the hatch, which was now face down on whatever structure they had inadvertently destroyed.

"Very sorry," he murmured.

"Quite all right," she said, squirming.

He wondered if they could manage to roll the craft by throwing their weight into one side, but the crowd that had gathered outside saved them the awkward effort.

They rolled again, this time sending Sophia on top of him. The hatch flipped open and a British sepoy tried to glower at them, but only succeeded in looking alternatively incredulous and amused. Ravi gave an embarrassed little wave.

He tried to assist Sophia out of the machine, succeeding only in managing to avoid hitting her foot with his face.

Ravi climbed out next. Crushed fruit littered the street, along with remnants of a wooden cart. An angry man, who Ravi took to be the fruit vendor, stood shaking his fist and muttering.

The crowd had grown quite large, most of them blinking in confusion, but there was some scattered clapping. A group of soldiers and sepoys, however, pointed weapons at them.

"Why," asked Ravi, "Are people always pointing guns at me?"

"Ravi Mukherjee?" one of them asked.

Ravi nodded.

"You are under arrest, on the order of Major Maxwell Cullen."

Ravi sighed.

****

Cullen paced outside Ravi's cell, wearing a self-satisfied grin, equal parts pompous and predatory.

"Theft of an airship belonging to the Crown. Destruction of property. Negligence resulting in the death of a worker. Blatant disregard of a direct order from the minister of Cape colony," Cullen recited, counting on his fingers as he did so.

Ravi said nothing. It would not matter to Cullen that the only item on his list actually his fault was the last. More to the point, it was not his fault that Elizabeth Cullen was who she was, or that she found Ravi attractive.

He found himself falling into his old habit of humoring Cullen by listening politely. It occurred to Ravi that it had never gotten him anywhere.

"You've certainly managed to rack up your list of crimes since we last met, haven't you, Mucker-jee?" Cullen continued. "And that's not even including your incompetence in my service."

Now that was just too much. "I am sure," said Ravi, "that your department runs much more smoothly since I have been away."

Cullen looked taken aback. "As a matter of fact," he sputtered. "It has!" He hesitated long enough for Ravi to know he was lying, and couldn't resist a self-satisfied smirk of his own. Cullen flushed. He opened his mouth to speak, closed it again, and reopened it, when a young assistant ran in, holding a telegram.

"Sir," he said, looking as if he might vomit at any moment. Cullen was so angry, however, that he missed the sick urgency in the assistant's voice.

"Mucker-jee, I warned you," he said, ignoring the young man, whose eyes widened in alarm. "I promised that if you ever set foot in Calcutta again you'd regret it. I intend to keep that promise."

"Sir!" the assistant said again, stepping between Cullen and the cell, which was rather difficult, since Cullen was nearly pressed up against the bars.

"What?" Cullen shouted at him.

"A second telegram from London. It says it's urgent, sir. Please take this."

"I'll find you when I'm through," Cullen responded.

The assistant shifted uneasily from one foot to the other, unsure how to proceed.

"It won't be long!" said Cullen. "Go on."

The assistant shook his head and slunk away.

Cullen turned back to Ravi. "I intend to see to it that you never see the outside of a jail cell again," he said. "And that's if you're lucky."

A shadow fell across Cullen and the bars of Ravi's cell as another figure entered. Cullen had his back to him, but Ravi could see him plainly. In that moment, Ravi's years of experience keeping his expression blandly polite in the face of Cullen's speeches finally paid off.

The figure cleared his throat.

"Later!" he shouted. "How many times do I have to tell you?"

Cullen wheeled to find Lord Curzon, Viceroy of India, standing in the doorway.

"You have received the telegrams from London, I trust?" the Viceroy asked. "Because I assure you that I have."

Ravi had never seen Cullen so aghast. He stood, flummoxed, as if he could gather up the words he had just spoken and cram them back in his mouth.

"Her Majesty is not amused," Curzon continued. "Therefore I am not amused. I hope you fully appreciate the gravity of that situation."

"Yes, sir. Of course, sir," Cullen stammered. "This man is a criminal, sir, spent some years in my service—"

"This man is an international hero who has received a personal invitation to Buckingham Palace from Her Majesty. Guards!"

Two guards stepped forward. Ravi recognized them, and knew that they had no great love for Major Cullen.

"Release this man immediately. Get him whatever he may require."

As they retrieved the key to Ravi's jail cell, Curzon turned back to Cullen. "I think it best if you stay out of my sight for a while," he said.

He turned to leave. Halfway to the door he turned around and gave Cullen a look of utter contempt. "A very long while."

When Curzon had gone, Ravi smiled pleasantly at Cullen and left.

****

Before Ravi was blinded by flashbulbs, he saw Hiram's tattered airship sinking in the Hooghly. He craned his neck in an attempt to see if anyone was sinking along with it, perhaps crying for help, but now he could see nothing but swirls of light and the vague outlines of people's hats. People were asking him questions, he knew, but they were all talking over each other, so he could barely make any of them out.

"—was it like?" came one voice.

"Utterly terrifying," responded Ravi. It occurred to him then that this was not a quote for the papers.

Before he could amend it, however, Sophia managed to squeeze through the crowd and threw her arms around his neck. A flashbulb went off.

"Thank God you are okay!" She said.

A new clamor of questions rose up about the nature of their relationship. Ravi could not answer, being unsure himself, though for the first time he considered proposing. He was aware that he would not be Major Westbridge's choice for a son-in-law, but Sophia had made it clear that she would not allow her father to make up her mind for her about such things.

"That, I suppose, is up to the lady," said Ravi.

Sophia smiled warmly. Was that encouragement? He would not know until they could be alone.

The sound of heavy wet feet came thundering toward them, as if a walrus had put on footwear and taught itself to run.

Hiram jostled his way through the crowd, sopping wet. He clasped Ravi's hand and pumped so hard Ravi wondered if he was trying to fill him with air like a bicycle tire.

"Ha!" Shouted Hiram. "We did it, m'boy! We did it, indeed!"

Hiram put on his best grin for the cameras, all the while shaking Ravi's hand.

Ravi should not have been at all surprised to see Gunter Wolfe plod through the crowd, glowering. Not to be outdone, he elbowed his way over to Ravi, displacing Sophia. Flashbulbs went off.

"Who is that one?" a member of the crowd asked.

"I am Mister Codon's partner," Gunter said. Ravi, annoyed, stepped around him, clasping hands with Sophia once again.

"Was, you mean," said Hiram, still grinning.

"What is next?" someone asked.

"The Moon? Other planets? There is no limit to what we can accomplish!" said Hiram, in his orator's voice.

"And you, Mister Mukherjee?"

Ravi thought. "I think we've plenty to do here on Earth. For instance, using airships for delivery to the countryside," he said. Perhaps someone would listen to him, now.

He saw a few people write it down. It was a beginning.

****

In the coming weeks, it was clear that the papers wanted to make a hero out of someone, but they could not figure out whom. This heroic venture had been undertaken by a brusque Irishman, a non-white colonial, a woman, and a citizen of the German empire—currently Britain's most bitter rival. It was clear they would have vastly preferred a tan-clad pith helmeted military officer such as Sophia's father. In this capacity, at least, Sophia was not the Westbridge they had wanted.

The papers argued whether the rocket was British or German, or the product of a successful collaboration. Some argued that the venture was evidence that there need be no hostilities between Britain and Germany, that the two nations should form an alliance. Many of the British papers lauded Hiram and vilified Gunter, though in other nations, particularly Germany, it was more often vice-versa.

The papers in India, at least those written by and for Indians, began to fiercely advocate for self-rule. The English in India seemed oblivious to this—leastwise, they ignored it.

Ravi found it interesting that several of the London papers focused on either him or Sophia, while ignoring or at least downplaying the other. Journalists speculated about the implication of the first person in space being a woman, or what it meant for the future that the first man to fly a rocket was a non-white colonial. It was as if talking about both at the same time would just be too much.

The articles Ravi enjoyed most, however, were those which pointed out the similarities and differences between Hiram's rocket and Jules Verne's vision in *From the Earth to the Moon*. One of the journalists had managed to reach Mister Verne for comment.

Sophia, meanwhile, had been invited to study at the Sorbonne. Ravi could hardly propose after hearing this news. She wanted to become a physicist too badly for him to make her choose between marriage and her dream. She promised to write often. He promised to do the same.

Bemused, he sat outside the Kolkata hotel where he had temporarily taken up residence. So many people had asked him what was next for the project that he hadn't had time to think about what was next for himself. He honestly did not know.

"Well, you'll be happy to know that there's a proposal up to use airships for delivery," said Hiram, startling Ravi.

"I didn't hear you come in," he said.

"I'll make this brief," said Hiram. "The Crown has decided to continue my funding. I'm looking for a new partner. Interested?"

Ravi pondered.

"Now, my good man, how will you be my moral compass if you don't say yes?" said Hiram, eyes twinkling.

"Can a crazy man even have a moral compass?" asked Ravi. But he could do more good, and perhaps prevent more harm, indulging his curiosity and using his abilities than he could by moping around the hotel.

"What do you plan to accomplish?" asked Ravi.

"I told you on the savannah that day, don't you remember? To the Moon, in ten years' time!" said Hiram.

"Ten years, is it? We'd better start building a new factory complex," said Ravi.

"An existing one, south of Delhi, is in the process of being renovated," said Hiram.

"Here in India, then?" asked Ravi. Though Delhi would be much different than Kolkata, it would be less different than London. He would, of course, visit London at Her Majesty's invitation, but he had no desire to stay.

Hiram nodded.

"When do you plan to begin work?" asked Ravi.

Hiram smiled. A shadow fell across Ravi, followed by a rope ladder.

"As soon as we get there," said Hiram. "I hope you don't mind, I took the liberty of arranging transport. I assumed you'd say yes."

The airship hovering overhed was considerably smaller than the former, designed for personal transport rather than launching a rocket. He noticed that across the hull in bold black letters was the name, "Sophia."

"I thought you weren't in the habit of naming airships," said Ravi.

"I changed my mind," said Hiram.

"Well, you realize I now couldn't bear to crash this one," said Ravi.

"Then we'll have to avoid getting shot at!" said Hiram jovially.

"Don't," said Ravi, "You'll jinx this voyage."

Hiram guffawed.

As Ravi reached for the rope, he saw honey blonde tresses tumble over the side of the ship.

"Hello!" Sophia called down to him. "So you said yes, too?"

Ravi turned to Hiram.

"Hiram has been teaching me to pilot, for real this time!" she said.

Ravi looked up at her, and then peered at the letters spelling her name on the hull.

Sophia laughed. "It wasn't my idea, I promise!"

"It was when I named the dirigible that I realized I'd grown attached to the both of you," said Hiram.

"But what about the Sorbonne?" Ravi called.

"I will be like Edmund Halley and become an astrophysicist by traveling the world!" called Sophia. "Except they didn't have dirigibles in Halley's time."

Ravi turned back to Hiram.

"Both of you should be in the field," said Hiram. "Not in an office or a laboratory. Trust me, I've worked with people who belong in an office. She'd be bored out of her wits. And so would you."

Ravi felt like he should protest, but could not.

"You're welcome," said Hiram. "Well? Are you going to board, or stand here all day?"

Ravi climbed the rope.

Matt Pearson and Cate Caldwell

Matt Pearson and Cate Caldwell began their collaboration in 2008. They have written several screenplays together, and have been finalists in such contests as the *Page International Screenwriting Awards* and the *Creative World Awards*.

Matt, a member of the *Mars Society*, has published papers on space settlement topics which have been described by critics as "contrary to popular thought and common sense."

Cate, with a Ph.D. in English, has somehow managed to avoid food service and instead landed a job as a university administrator. She has published a smattering of short fiction along the way. *The Sun Never Sets* is both Matt and Cate's first published longer work.

When not writing, Matt and Cate enjoy hiking, backcountry camping, scuba diving, and having adventures. They live just north of Detroit in a dilapidated house built by a stone mason in the 1920s with a pride of super-genius attack cats who are too independent to behave like proper minions.

www.ingramcontent.com/pod-product-compliance
Lightning Source LLC
Chambersburg PA
CBHW072127170626
46813CB00004B/1721